I0745386

# CRICKETS

by

Lee Chappel

Bleau PRESS

*Crickets* is a work of fiction. Names, characters, places, and incidents are either products of the author's imagination or are used fictitiously. Any resemblance to actual events, businesses, locales, or persons, living or dead, is entirely coincidental.

2021 Bleau Press

All rights reserved.

ISBN 978-1-951796-07-5 (hardcover)
ISBN 978-1-951796-06-8 (paperback)
ISBN 978-1-951796-05-1 (ebook)

Cover design by Tom Anderson

# CRICKETS

# 1

*Kara*

I hear his voice.

My knees lock, and I wonder if I'll topple over, maybe hit my head on the edge of the tub this time and drown in the spray of the shower.

When I turn off the water, it's quiet again. Probably the pipes did it this time. Sometimes, my pipes still sound like Dalton Rolenfeld.

I step over the tub and lean against the wall to dry off before wrapping up in a robe. The hallway's dark, but I don't check the lock on the front door anymore when I pass by. This is why I picked a second story walkup, why I've stayed here for the last decade, hidden in these rows of identical 90's builds with brick fronts and bright white siding, this in-between place where Columbus runs into the cornfields that rush towards home. Here, the floodlights over the lawn stay on through the night, and I can watch the cars rumbling by on the freeway from my bedroom window.

Brent has a sitcom on by the time I get to the sofa. When I sit down, he lifts my feet over his knees, like we do, and we talk about work and people from home I don't really know anymore and how we'll spend the rest of his weekend here. These weekends together have all been about the same for us since we were twelve.

"You've been working from home a lot, haven't you?" he asks in the middle of a conversation I haven't been paying much attention to.

I look at my empty desk. I can just see the glowing blue dot of my laptop in its drawer. My papers are all filed away.

"You're not too busy," he adds.

"No." So I could go back anytime, he means, go home. It's almost time. My dad's celebration of life—that's what we're calling it, since we didn't have a funeral—is coming up.

"You know you could come home early. Kym's been saying we should go down to Cincinnati, and Leah..."

"Who?" I ask.

Brent looks at me, then back at the TV. "I told you about Leah, didn't I? Kym Hartmann's intern, the one who's got a thing for me? It's been driving Kym nuts."

"I don't think you did."

There's a pause, and I try to focus on the sitcom. It's one I'd know, I think, if I ever watched TV on my own. I recognize the actress from a show we used to watch.

"So Kym," I prompt.

Brent shifts, putting his feet up on the table. "I don't know," he says. "Maybe." He laughs, then. "I guess you thought I'd sworn to celibacy."

I laugh, too, but I guess I had, a little.

"It's because you feel safe here, isn't it?" he asks as soon as we're quiet again.

I look back at the TV. It's that I don't feel safe at home, he means, in Paige, that the woods around my dad's place are full of shadows for me.

"You still think about it sometimes, don't you?"

I shrug. But Brent knows my shrugs. "More now, I guess."

"Because of the election?"

"That's probably it."

"You've thought about saying something?" he asks.

"Again," I remind him, because I reported it when it happened—right away, like everyone says you're supposed to. I haven't changed my story.

Sometimes I want to. Sometimes, I want to tell them everything, to scream it from the rooftops before the election. But I know this wouldn't make a difference. Mine's just one of those stories that can't be true.

# 2



*Detective Sam Ellis*

"Don't be gettin' any ideas now, Ellis."

I pull my eyes away from the old box TV strapped to the ceiling in the corner of the room. Nate Stubsen's towering over my desk.

"Ideas?" I ask.

"About Dalton."

I look back at the news, at Dalton Rolenfeld's face. There's a smaller picture of his father, the current Senator Robert Rolenfeld, next to his. They say Dalton looks just like him, but I don't see it. Dalton's features are finer, more delicate. His smile's wider, too, and his hair's a shade lighter, like the lanky woman in the background who must be his mom. She's always a step or two behind him and never says anything.

"I won't," I say.

Stubsen tries to perch on my desk, setting a thigh across the corner behind my computer tower. "Come on," he says. "It's every girl in Paige, with him. Prolly the whole state now."

I don't remind him I'm not a girl anymore, or from Paige. I

stick out enough as it is between all these big, blonde men with buzz cuts.

Stubsen slides off the desk a little, and I look back at the TV. My desk's a new addition in the middle of the room—straight from Rolenfeld Industries—and some of the other guys still run into it when they're not paying attention. Stubsen never does, though. He's always looking at me.

"I was wondering about Dalton's teeth," I say. "Where'd he get those done?"

"His teeth?"

"Veneers."

Stubsen twists to look at the screen. "Man, you do see stuff."

Not that it's much use here; personalities are manufactured in this town like desks and beds, so everyone in Paige reads as at least a little fake to me.

"Howard Lange would've done 'em. He's got that dental place downtown. Big deal, was in a magazine and everything."

"Really?" I ask. "I've got to learn all these names."

I watch the headlines roll across the bottom of the screen as Stubsen goes on about the Lange family. They're all connected, of course, like these Paige families are. Parker Lange, the dentist's daughter, dated Dalton Rolenfeld in high school. And these connections matter, even the casual ones you wouldn't expect to mean anything.

I'm remembering some names now, but I don't have all the local families down yet. I should, I know; a ticket to a Rolenfeld or a Lange could end my career faster than all the bullets whizzing around Whitehall. Paige is still getting used to me, too, to an officer they don't call "sir."

I lean back in my chair. "I keep thinking I've heard of Rolenfeld somewhere else," I say.

"Well, he's been on the TV since..."

"No. That's not it. Was there a case? I thought I saw something when I was looking through the files." I told the others I was getting to know the town's history—they're all so proud of it—when I spent my first week rummaging through the boxes in the back room. There's always a backlog of cases in little towns like this, and going through them's the fastest way to find out what you're getting into.

"Which one?" Stubsen asks.

"Wasn't Dalton the one with Peterson's daughter..."

"Sheriff Stan? I forgot you knew him."

"I interviewed with him." I didn't get the job until he was dead, though, until Baer was instated. "So I think it was about ten years ago," I say. "His daughter's name was on something, wasn't it? Like a rape or something? Is that even close?"

"Yeah." Stubsen straightens, leaning towards me. "Right on. That was Dalton. Or at least that's what Kara said."

"You think she was lying?"

He shifts, scooting my computer tower to the side. "Well, you can see why she'd make up somethin' like that."

"Sure."

Stubsen winks. "Just don't go givin' Dalton a ticket or anything, okay?"

"Okay," I say, and think he might leave.

He doesn't. "You want some coffee?" he asks.

I lift my thermos full of tea. I haven't integrated it yet with all the guys' coffee mugs.

"Smart girl," Stubsen says. "Stuff's gonna kill me one day. It's what killed Sheriff Stan, you know."

I look at the clock. There are still ten minutes until shift starts. So Stubsen asks me about the rest of my weekend again, and I tell him I'm catching up on some things at the house tonight. I alternate this with visiting friends in Columbus when he asks.

"You really like workin' hard these Saturdays," he says when there's nothing else to say. "You're a worker bee."

I wait.

"Anyway, if you're gonna be here all day, I could use your help. If you have the time, I mean. There's some fence damage out on 261. I could really use a profiler."

I try to keep my face still. Stubsen imagines I'm his partner, I think, because the plaque on my desk says "detective" on it, too, and he watches a lot of police sitcoms—set in cities, not in places like this. He thinks I'm the one who reads people, and he's the one who takes them down. We're supposed to get together in the end.

"So you want me to profile a fence?" I ask.

He laughs—fake, too loud. "Two farmers," he says. "One family's newer. I don't know which of 'em's tellin' the truth about who ran into the chainlink between their places."

I agree and, a couple minutes later, watch him leave for patrol. When I look back at the TV, the news has gone to weather.

# 3



*Kara*

I'm screaming into the darkness, but I swear I can see Dalton's eyes.

It's Brent's face, though, in the sliver of light from behind the curtains, his big brown orbs like a cocker spaniel, his long arms around me. I'm out of air. Maybe I really was screaming this time.

It takes a few minutes for all the sound in my head to stop, but then it's quiet. Brent doesn't say anything as I catch my breath. He knows it can take me a while to come back to normal.

I lean back against the headboard and go through my exercise, counting things I can hear and see and smell like my first therapist taught me, the one I started seeing just after it happened, when I thought this was something I might be able to hear or see or smell away.

I can only hear my breathing. Brent's must be quieter. I can smell our pizza from earlier and the Indian takeout we had for lunch. I can smell my sweat, too, like usual after these nights, and Brent, the way he's always smelled, like the deodorant he's worn at least since he stayed with us in seventh grade and the laundry detergent his mom's used forever.

He reaches for the lamp on my nightstand, and then I can see, too—my dresser, the bump under the covers that's my body all twisted up with the duvet, the open door to the hallway and his sheet that's slipped off the corner of the pullout sofa.

"This one was different," I say when I have my voice back.

"The nightmare?"

I nod.

"It's because Dalton's been on TV so much. You have to expect it's gonna happen sometimes."

"I heard crickets."

I don't have to look at him to know the expression on Brent's face.

"Just this time," I tell him. "It hasn't happened before. There were crickets this time. Everything else was the same."

He twists, looks over towards the window, where the streetlights are barely peeking through the gauzy curtains. "There are probably still some outside. Maybe when you were waking up..."

"No. It was the whole time."

Brent doesn't say anything. I guess there's not much to say. This is a flashback to something ten years ago I probably don't remember anything else right from, either. They warn you that can happen, that when your brain fills in the gaps, the story it creates doesn't always make sense.

"Could you *see* anything new?" he asks after a minute.

"No. Just Dalton." And he's the same every time, with that weird smile on his face as he hovers over me in the darkness. It's the look he had when he grabbed me. It never changed.

"And all you heard were crickets?" Brent asks.

"And Sebastian." It was the only thing Dalton said during it—the only thing I heard, anyway, so it's the same in every nightmare. I still don't know who he was talking to.

This is what therapists call an obsession. It's natural to have one after something like this. It gives us something to focus on, something productive to think about, some little mystery to solve. But it's no good for me now, after years with no answers. By this point, I'm supposed to have come to terms with not knowing what Dalton really said.

Brent runs a hand down my back, the way he has since failed cheerleader tryouts in sixth grade, when he started calling me "Ra Ra" as a joke. Because I should have been a cheerleader, he said. But Brent's always thought things should have gone better for me.

"Why don't we go out for a walk tomorrow," he says. "Maybe being outside'll help."

"Yeah. Thanks," I say, then, "I'm sorry."

He sits up and tugs at the duvet, trying to find the corner. "It sucks that you're still having these. It can't help being alone here all the time."

"It's usually okay," I tell him, and mean it. I don't know why the dreams come back when I'm not expecting them to, and when I have someone here, even. Maybe it really is just the election coverage. This is the first nightmare I've had in months, maybe in a year.

"I think you should tell someone," Brent says after a minute of quiet.

"A therapist?"

"No, I mean like a cop. About the crickets. That isn't in the report, is it?"

I shake my head. Dalton was in the report, though. I thought at the time they shouldn't need anything else. Maybe I still think that. I don't know for sure there was another person in that room.

Brent pulls the duvet up over my chest. "We have a lady officer now. I told you that, didn't I? Mom met her at The Strawberry. She's with Cody Muller. You could talk to her, tell her what you remembered."

"Heard," I correct. Because you can't say 'remembered' with things like this. "And that makes me sound crazy."

"You don't sound crazy." But Brent's always said that, too.

"I heard crickets. It was December."

We're quiet for a while then, and I sit forward and try to unroll the covers around my feet. I don't know how I do it, how I kick the sheets tighter and tighter around my calves until I can't move them at all.

"Let's watch a movie," Brent says once I'm sitting up again. "We might as well. We're both awake."

I agree, and he goes to get his laptop.

I only make it through the first couple scenes of one of those 90's romcoms that are all the same and wake up with my head on Brent's chest and sunlight streaming in through the curtains.

4

*Sam*

Sunday morning, I have my usual brunch with Cody Muller at The Strawberry, an old diner with red leather booths that always smell like bacon and feel too hot in the sun. This place is the central hub of Paige, and our brunches are Cody's way of showing the rest of the town that I belong here.

Our waitress touches his arm when she greets us, a gesture I've gotten used to. We come between the two major church seatings, St. Luke's at 8:30 and St. Mark's at 11, when it's quiet, but there are always some back claps and nods and the occasional handshake for Cody. I'm still learning the social dialect of this place, which gestures mean something and which don't.

As she sets out the toast they always bring first and takes our orders, the waitress's attention is glued to Cody, to his gray eyes and sandy hair she probably called *dreamy* back in high school. He was a football star then. Now he's a local business owner, so he hasn't lost any status. He opened his own construction company a few years back and says it's been a slow growth thing, but it seems like he's already done work on a third of the houses in this town.

So it's not just his history here that makes him helpful; he knows the *insides* of all these lives in a way you wouldn't get even from years of living and working around them.

"Well?" I ask when she goes away, because we haven't had this one before.

He picks up his coffee mug. "Madison Fuhs. A couple years behind me in school. Went to U of L. Dance team."

I watch Madison disappear behind the partition. Six months ago, I thought I could read faces, but Paige is full of looks like the one she's been giving me, and you have to know so much more to be able to interpret them.

"Dance team," I echo. "So was the Rolenfeld kid in your year?"

"A year ahead."

I open one of the little honey packets for my tea. They say all the honey here's local, like the chicken from the processing plant down by the river, but the packets aren't labeled. "What's he like?" I ask.

Cody meets my eyes, his brow coming together how it does when he's thinking. "I'm not voting for him," he says, "if that's what you mean."

"Not a good guy?"

"You have a case."

I don't know how he knows it's not just the senate seat I'm wondering about. I haven't said anything about cases to Cody before, but I know the other cops don't follow the same rules; a little scandal's everywhere in Paige before it even hits the scanners.

"Not officially," I admit. "But there's an old one I have been kind of wondering about."

"You're thinkin' of Kara Peterson, I bet, Sheriff Stan's daughter."

I try a bite of my toast. It's pumpernickel here and always tastes a little stale to me. "You know her?"

Cody nods, drinking his coffee. "She was a year ahead of me. In Dalton's class."

"Were you friends?"

"No. I was a shop rat."

"And she was…"

"Bright. And not into football. She was in law school when it happened, I think."

"Right." That's what Stubsen said, too. What he said, actually, was that Kara would have known just what to say to get someone like Dalton in trouble.

"Tell me about her?" I ask.

"I believe her."

I look across the table and study Cody's face. When I first met him on the side of the highway with a flat tire and two weeks to find a place here to live, I thought he was just a smoother kind of Stubsen, part of Paige's good ol' boys club. But he's brighter than he lets on, and he seems to read people well. So if I'm going to trust anyone's take on a local, it's his.

"What else?" I ask.

"Her mom died. Cancer, I think it was, when she was in high school. She's close with her neighbor, Brent Thomas. His mom, Bev, took care of her and Stan when it happened."

I look out the window, at the leaves starting to drop from the big oak in the median. Sometimes I think time goes by too slowly here, that we should be through winter and into spring already. But I only took the job a little over four months ago. "I think I might have met Bev," I say.

Cody nods. "Nurse at the hospital. She's the one with the sleeves under her scrubs, got a big scar on her arm from an accident years back."

"Married?"

"Her husband died, too. Think Brent woulda been in middle school then."

"Bad luck," I say, like some people say about rape kits that don't get run.

When our breakfast gets here—quickly, like always—Cody plows through a couple thick strips of Canadian bacon as he waits for me to say more.

"So you think Dalton would have done something like that?" I ask after a while.

"I think Dalton'd do whatever he thought he could get away with," Cody says.

I think about this, and we talk about sociopaths for a bit. We have a laugh when he says something about Jack the Ripper, but of course the problem with sociopaths is that they have real names, too, normal names. You never see them coming.

When Madison starts hovering again, wiping down the table next to ours, we change the subject to the Christmas festival on the square, and Cody has another cup of coffee as I finish my eggs.

He gets the check before I can, ignoring my protest like always.

Because his mom would have his hide otherwise, he says, and I'm probably the only civil servant in the county not on the take. I haven't been here long enough, I guess he means.

By the time we walk out into the parking lot, there's a line of cars from St. Mark's in the turn lane, and I follow Cody to his truck. The house I'm renting is close enough to walk to, but it's cooler out today and cloudy. Some early leaves are tumbling around on the sidewalks.

It would have been cold just before Christmastime at that party at the Rolenfeld place. Everyone would have been inside. There were so many people in the house, someone had to have seen something. And Kara's statement was that she heard something Dalton said, like he was talking to another person in the room. There must have been at least one witness, someone the report missed.

"You're thinkin' again," Cody says as we pull out into Main Street. "It's that look you got when you couldn't decide if you cared about your screened-in porch gettin' fixed or torn down."

"It's the case," I tell him before I can think better of it. "Is there anyone else? Who would have been at Dalton's party that night, I mean?"

"Loads of people. Most of 'em probably pretty toasted."

Of course. This is a drinking town. "Is there anyone you think could have been part of it? Who you'd think of, I mean, other than Dalton?"

Cody slows down as the gravel of my driveway crunches under his tires. "I think it's right up Dalton's alley," he says after a couple seconds. "But as for anybody else, it's hard to say. If she said somebody else was there, I'd believe her, even if it was somebody I'd thought was okay."

"It would have been someone you knew," I say. But that's just how these cases go. It's always someone you know.

# 5



*Kara*

When I wake up again later on Sunday morning, the sun's high over my window, and other side of my bed's cool, the duvet pulled back.

I hear some noise from the kitchen—Brent making pancakes, scraping at a mixing bowl and setting out pans. It takes me back to Sunday mornings in his mom's kitchen when we were teenagers, after his dad and my mom were both gone, back to talking Mario Kart shortcuts over the batter hissing on the coils of the stove as the breeze blew in through the screen door so we wouldn't set off the smoke alarm.

I throw a fuzzy robe over my pajamas, because it's getting to be that time of year, and pull my hair into a clip.

I find Brent standing over the range I never use. "You feeling okay?" he asks when he sees me.

"Fine."

"Good." But this is how it goes, with your best friend; after a while, they know what all your variations of 'fine' mean.

"Does it happen a lot?" he asks. "The nightmare?"

"Not a lot. And never like last night. There hasn't been anything new in it before." But I guess that's the difference between a nightmare and a memory, the way a nightmare can always change, can always get worse.

"It's bothering you again," he says. "I mean, things are getting bad for you again."

I sit down at the island and reach for the bag of chocolate chips he's left out for me, a brand from Gleson's I can never find here in the city.

"It's probably just stress," I say. There's always a reason these things pop up again when you think they're gone. And there's plenty for me to be stressed about, I think, after my dad.

"Does it help to talk about it?"

"No. I just want to understand."

"The crickets?"

"That, and Sebastian. It's that it doesn't make sense." If it did, I wouldn't have to think about it, and it wouldn't cause nightmares—not once a year, not once a decade, not ever. That's what I imagine, anyway, that once I understand it, it won't bother me anymore. I don't know how I'm supposed to accept what happened to me until I have all the answers, until I know the things I'm supposed to forget.

I take a sip of the coffee Brent's already poured me, too bitter, and think back to the whipped cream drinks I used to love back then, mochas and frappuccinos from the place in the basement of the campus dining hall. I can't remember when I stopped drinking them. I guess that's another thing that's changed about me without my noticing. It's like I stepped into a new person that night and don't have a complete memory of who I used to be.

"You've got everything in order for the dinner?" Brent asks, his back to me now.

I walk over to the window and watch a bunch of cars on the freeway, little flashes in the sun as they pass by. "I think so," I say.

"You're doing really well."

I don't know how to respond, I guess because I don't know what 'well' means. It seems like if I really were doing well, just thinking about my dad's dinner wouldn't make me want to cry. I've grieved, and it's been a few months. It was a while before that, I guess, probably around the time Mom died when I was just turning fifteen, that my dad wasn't a big part of my life anymore. That's what friends are for, and neighbors.

Brent doesn't say anything as he takes up my pancake and drowns it in maple syrup.

I get a fork and sit down again. "It doesn't make sense," I say when he hands me the plate, because I can't help it. "I still can't think of any Sebastians. It couldn't have been someone who knew me."

Brent goes back to the stove, to the next pancake that's almost ready—his, with blueberries instead of chocolate chips already mixed in, dark lumps bubbling on the surface. "And Dalton did?" he asks.

"Dalton and I knew each other, at least. He was in our class. We'd talked."

"That's your lawyer brain," Brent says. Except it's not a

lawyer's brain, not exactly; it's an *almost* lawyer's brain that's probably never going to be a lawyer, a brain that was put on hold a decade ago.

"You keep looking for reasons," he continues, "like you would've had if you'd done something like this. But he...you can't assume he thinks like you do."

"But why? Why *me?*"

Brent shrugs as he slides his pancake onto a plate. "The opportunity presented itself, I guess. You were alone. He was there. There's no telling what he thought."

"Dalton," I say, because it was Dalton who grabbed me, Dalton whose voice I heard, Dalton who I've seen and heard every time since then.

Brent doesn't respond to this, because the only thing I know for sure, other than Dalton saying "Sebastian," are the green numbers on a bedside alarm clock. And Dalton was outside, just under his father's security camera and making out with Parker Lange at 11:10 that night. And anyway, Dalton's untouchable.

Maybe this is why I want so badly for it to be someone else, to throw out everything my eyes and ears told me that night. Maybe this is all about wanting and nothing about the truth.

I take another sip of coffee, and Brent pulls out his barstool.

"You didn't really think it was planned, did you?" he asks.

I shake my head and use my fork to plow some syrup off my pancake.

I want to say that I *do* think it was planned, though, that I know it was. But that's because my story isn't all truth, either.

That afternoon, Brent and I grab a late lunch at a cafe down the block and walk around the too-blue pond on the other side of the highway for a little while. Things are right again, I think, normal—*safe*, like I always feel here, with the wind blowing the shampoo smell through my hair and the trees starting to turn yellow.

So I don't think anything of the mail I pick up on our way back. Brent's collecting his dop kit from the bathroom when I find the blank envelop on top of the stack.

The rest is magazines, mostly, and mailers, a couple bills I always pay online and something from Miami of Ohio's alumni association, splashes of red and white on shiny cardstock. I don't go for the blank envelope right away, and I'm not ready when I open it.

Inside is a picture, a little grayed down, like you'd print from home. It's my apartment. I can see the top of the toaster oven and my mug of tea out in the living room. It's looking in through the kitchen window. The light from my laptop's reflected on the mug; my feet must be just a couple inches away.

There's a slip of paper behind the picture with just two words: *I'll win.*


A few minutes later, I'm sitting on the linoleum, and Brent's standing behind me reading the note. Even though it's just two words. Maybe I shouldn't be on the linoleum from a picture and just two words.

"It's not exactly a threat, is it?" I say as I stand up. There's still a little cold coffee in the carafe from this morning, and I pour it into a new mug.

Brent slams the paper down on the island like it's something heavier, something real. "You have to show it to somebody," he says. "You've got to turn it in."

"I guess." But it was just two words. And what could two words do, to someone who says they're so okay?

"He's messing with you again. And he was *here* this time, right..." Brent jabs a finger at the window.

I don't say anything. I don't know what to say. This is all a game to Dalton, what he did, and then this, whatever happens next.

"Why?" I ask after a few sips of coffee, as Brent's pacing back and forth on the other side of the island. Because this is just another part of my story that doesn't fit, that isn't right.

He stops and looks out the window, like Dalton might be there now. The picture was at night. You can see the dark window on the other side of the living room.

"He's trying to intimidate you. And now he knows where you live. Alone, without anybody even around to..."

"Why?" I repeat.

"Maybe he thinks you're gonna say something at the last minute. Before the election."

I nod like I understand this, but what *could* I say, at this point, that would make a difference? I told the police everything they needed to know. I don't have any cards left to play.

I pick up the piece of paper again and read it like I might have missed something before in these two words. Then I take another gulp of coffee. I don't know when I started being able to drink it cold. "You're sure it's Dalton, then," I say.

Brent sits down again. I look past him.

"Who else?" he asks. When I don't answer, he asks me to come home with him. "Go to The Strawberry and Gleson's," he says. "Let Dalton know he doesn't scare you. Have someone at least *around*."

And then he has a plan, like he always does. He'll stay the night here so he can drive me home. We'll get to the house when it's still light out tomorrow. My dad's truck is there waiting for me, still insured. Brent's put gas in it and driven it around some to keep the battery going.

"What about your work tomorrow?" I ask.

He shakes his head, squinting towards the window. "Not a big deal," he says. "I'll email. I have plenty of days. And you definitely shouldn't be here alone." He comes over then and puts an arm around me. "You can do this," he tells me. "You're safe."

I nod and agree, because I want to believe him.

6

Monday morning, they eat another round of pancakes, going through the last of the chocolate chips, and wait out the early workday traffic before taking 77 North to Paige. There are only a few rows of townhomes and half acre developments sprawling out into the country they pass before hitting the cornfields.

Kara's head's against the passenger door, and she's wearing her sunglasses today. She doesn't take them off even when they reach the cloud bank at the county line. She knows this road still, the way the cornfields give way to power lines that dip into a valley the storms always cling to. It feels darker here, the hills around the county pushing in on it.

Rolenfeld Industries welcomes them to Paige with a big stone marker in the shadow of the factory. Its parking lots are full like always on a Monday. Nothing's changed here.

Kara looks for something in her purse as they pull onto Main Street, pass The Strawberry and the new ice cream place on the square her dad told her about the last time she called. She looks up in time to see her middle school and the bait and ammo shop on the corner leading out to Baker's lake.

It takes another five minutes of the road sliding down into the woods for them to pass the big lawn at the base of the Rolenfeld's mansion. It's just another minute, then, to Brent's place and her dad's—right around the corner from the Rolenfeld's, really, but if feels farther. They park in the gravel of what's her driveway now, and Brent follows her inside.

Stan's coffee machine's still plugged in on the counter. There are probably old grounds in the filter, unless someone thought to clean them out when he passed. A few people have been in and out of the house—Baer, the new sheriff, and Bev, Brent's mom, who's had keys to this place since before Kara can remember.

The cuckoo clock on the wall—a gift from just before the Rolenfelds stopped making them—is still going, just a little dusty. The TV remote's sitting out on the arm of the sofa.

Kara collapses into what used to be her chair at the kitchen table and starts crying before Brent can think of what to say.

# 7

*Kara*

The first few days at my dad's house go slowly—like wadin' through molasses, as he used to say, because he liked to remind us he was born in Kentucky.

It's not just all the things that need to be cleared out, though; it feels like anything can stop me here, can halt a run of progress. There are little fragments of the childhood I almost don't remember every time I reach under a bed or open a drawer. I don't know why I thought things would be different, that this place would have changed like I have.

Wednesday afternoon, Brent's at work, and Bev's downstairs folding a pile of Dad's almost identical black coats from the entry closet while I clean out the master bath. You wouldn't think there would be so much to go through in a man's bathroom, but it's like decades have built up in here, settled into the backs of the drawers and fallen down between the cabinets. There are even traces of my mom still, maxi pads stuck behind the pipes under the sink and an empty box of her hair dye folded neatly under some toilet paper.

Bev comes into the doorway as I'm scooping the last of the bottles from the vanity into a trash bag.

"You doing okay?" she asks.

"Good," I tell her, and try to sound like it. I forget sometimes what this used to sound like for me. But Brent's probably already told her about my appointment at the station tomorrow, so maybe she doesn't expect me to be *good*, exactly. "I really appreciate this."

"It's nothing," Bev says, her usual. This is one of those times I wish I could be like her, how her face and her body never let on what's going on inside. She doesn't seem any different today than on all our pancake mornings or for graduations or funerals or even for that period after her accident when we were twelve. I remember the day Brent and I were finally allowed to see her once her bruises had all faded to green, how she laughed at something one of the other nurses said and then, afterwards, put on a long-sleeved shirt under her scrubs and went right back to looking normal again. She was back at work on the same floor the day after the hospital discharged her.

"You should eat something," she says. And I guess she knows best; she's done this routine of clearing out before, after her husband died, and then she spent the couple years of my mom's cancer nursing her and doing it all over again, hauling her things away and taking care of me and my dad.

I fish my phone out of my pocket. It's seven. I had some of the lasagna she brought over this morning—it's the same, too—but I should be hungry by now. I didn't notice it getting dark out.

"I'm pretty stuffed." This is an automatic response, a routine Bev and I had established by the time my mom got really sick.

"You need to keep your strength up." She says it the way people say it here, Germans who think you can regenerate, body and soul, whenever you really want to.

So I follow her downstairs with the bag of trash. She turns on the TV, switching off the local news right away. After flipping through the guide for a little bit, she lands on a house-hunting show. Maybe she can tell I'm not sleeping well, that I need more good voices in this house. Brent's probably told her about the nightmare, or maybe this is just what she expects to happen now I'm home and surrounded by all Dad's things. Maybe this is what normal grief looks like.

As we eat more of her lasagna and steamed vegetables, Bev brings up the gala next Saturday for the county humane society, the one Dad always MC'd.

"It would help get your mind off things," she says.

I look around the kitchen. There are random piles of nic nacs along the island and a group of mugs collecting dust over by the coffee machine. I don't know why Dad had so many mugs; he always used the same one.

"I wouldn't have anything to wear," I tell her.

Bev starts folding placemats on the corner of the table. "Course you do," she says. "All those dresses up in your room. You're still the same size, aren't you? Or we could go shopping. That might be fun."

I set aside my lasagna and try a bite of carrot cake. It tastes dry, but maybe it's just because it's been in the fridge for the last couple days. Bev's carrot cakes were always my favorite. She took over the recipe from my mom.

"Just think about it," she says.

I agree, and she lets this go for now.

After we're finished with the dishes, she puts on her jacket and tries to convince me the house will start to feel better soon.

"I'll call you in the morning," she says, "and come by with lunch, okay?"

I thank her.

There's a stack of magazines in a plastic bag at the door that she forgets when she leaves. I almost ignore it, until I remember I don't have anything else to read, anything else to do here, really, but wade through all these things I don't want to remember.

I drop the first magazine as soon as I pull it out of the bag. Maybe I was expecting *Oprah* or *Southern Living*, like my mom used to read. I wasn't expecting women—girls, really. They look too young to be women.

Bev comes back in then. "I forgot..." she says, and bends down to pick up the magazine. "Sorry. I was just gonna throw those out for you."

She drops it into the bag with the others and doesn't meet my eyes. She looks uncomfortable, I think, like maybe we should be uncomfortable.

"Sorry, Kara," she says again. "I should have gotten all that out before you came home." There's a pause. "It's like that in every house, you know."

"Why are they so young?"

"Oh," she says, tying the top of the bag shut, sealing them in, but I can still see the covers through the plastic. "It's all like that, American porn."

"Right."

"This'll all feel better soon," she promises, and gives me a long hug before she goes, this time with the plastic bag.

*　　*

The next morning, I'm looking out the window at the station as I suck in deep breaths like there's not enough oxygen in this room. It hasn't changed, either; these blinds have always listed a little to the right, and the view to the parking lot's the same except that the trees in the median are all a little taller and Baer's new SUV is in my dad's parking spot. I still know everything else here—the smell of the coffee they never change the filter on, the hard chairs, the desk where I bumped my forehead when I was four and needed my first stitches.

I turn when Samantha Ellis comes through the doorway. She's new, but Baer thought I'd feel better talking with her than with any of the guys.

She smiles as she introduces herself—Sam, she says—and reaches for my hand. She's pretty, about my age with dark hair and a cut you can tell didn't come from Paige, a blunt bob that ends at her shoulders.

I wonder how she's been getting along here, sticking out the way a woman probably always will in this building, as I try to return her smile. Then we make small talk about fall in Ohio and how quickly the weather changes this time of year and how the local stations always get it wrong. There's a sort of bubble around Paige that doesn't follow any of the usual satellite rules.

"You have something new, the sheriff thought," she says when we've run out of these things to talk about.

It takes me a second to process this, to remember Baer's the sheriff now. I get Dalton's note out of my purse.

Sam takes her time with it, studying the words like I did, like more of them might suddenly show up there.

"No return address?"

"No." I hand her the picture, but she doesn't have to look at it long to know I'm not in it. I'm just out of the frame, I want to tell her—I have to be, since my tea's out and you can see the light from my laptop reflected on the mug—but I know this isn't worth anything. I could have taken the picture as easily as I could have written the note. She doesn't have any reason to believe me.

"Getting these must have been really upsetting," she says when she finally sets them back on the table. "When did they come?"

"Sunday. They were with my mail, but I hadn't checked it for a few days."

She nods. I think she's going to ask why I didn't report this sooner, but she doesn't, instead saying she wants to fill out some paperwork for submitting more evidence for my case. I nod along. I don't know if they'll take this seriously, now there's something you can hold. It seems wrong to me that they might take a note and a picture seriously when they didn't a rape.

"Would you be willing to go through it all with me?" Sam asks.

"One more time, if you're up to..."

"Sure."

"Just because I'm new here. So I'm kind of behind the ball, you know."

"Of course."

When she gets up to get the papers, she's careful not to scrape her chair against the tile. That one always catches on the grout line. "Can I get you something?" she asks. "Tea? Coffee?"

I shake my head and thank her. Once the door closes, I try to focus back out the window, on some leaves blowing off the big sycamore in front of the movie theater. I count things I can see—the tree and the new playground equipment towering over the old seesaw, the bench by the walking path that winds around by the river and the bridge that's always covered in spiny sweet gum balls this time of year. I tell myself I should feel safe in this building, in these places I know, but my hands are sweaty when I dig around in my purse for some lip balm.

Sam comes back a minute later and sits quietly across from me as I fill out a form for submitting new evidence. It's not one of the papers I've seen before, but things have probably changed a lot since I've spent time here. I used to imagine my dad running a dusty office in the Wild West and thought he was elected sheriff because he pulled off the look best.

This form's simple, and it turns out it's easier to write about the note and the picture—when and how I found them, what the envelope looked like—than it is to think about what they might mean.

When I'm finished, we sit quietly for a few minutes as Sam thumbs through the case report in an old manila file folder like the ones Dad used to keep on his desk.

"I don't mean to bring this up for you again," she says. "You've thought about it a lot, I bet, in the last decade."

"I have, yeah."

"And you're confident you saw Dalton."

"Saw him and heard him."

She turns back a page. "That's right. He was talking to someone. It's in the statement you gave at the hospital."

"Sebastian."

She lifts her head. "Sebastian?"

"That's what Dalton said," I tell her. "Or what I thought he said. I told them at the hospital."

Sam looks at me for a second, then clicks her pen and starts writing. "It must be in the original notes," she says, "but it's good to have it in here, too, with this copy. Do you know anyone named Sebastian?"

"No."

"No," she echoes, sitting back in her chair. "No one at the party with a nickname, maybe, or a name that sounds the same?"

"Not who I've remembered."

"And you hadn't seen anyone hanging around your apartment before Sunday? Nothing unusual?"

I shake my head and almost say something about the crickets. But I know I wouldn't take someone seriously if they told me they'd heard crickets in December. "No."

"And there's no one you can think of who might have wanted..." She stops short of saying what you can't say about rape, whatever it is those people want.

"No," I say.

"No grudges, no old high school rivalries or anything like that, that might have festered while you were away?"

"No." There's nothing. I must have gone through every man I know in this town a dozen times over the last decade.

Sam nods and closes the file. "Okay," she says. "I want to review all this. I'm really sorry for everything you've been through, and I want you to know that I'm taking it seriously."

I thank her, and I can't tell yet if she's as full of shit as the rest of them or not.

# 8

Sam

I minimize Kara Peterson's file on my screen when Stubsen comes through the double doors from the hallway. I watch him this time, really look at him and expect to see something there that I haven't seen before. He's the only Stubsen left in the county. I remember how quick he was to tell me when I met him, thinking he was a hot commodity.

"Hey there, Ellis," he says when he sees me. "Stayin' late again?"

I slide the form with Kara's handwriting into my top desk drawer. There's a little a gap you'd think was meant for hiding things. "Just wrapping up," I tell him.

He comes over like usual, and I pretend to look at the weekly schedule that's up on my computer. He stops just an inch too close and leans over my shoulder like he's reading the screen.

"You met with Sheriff Stan's daughter today, didn't you?"

"Kara? That's right."

"Did she remember something new, or..."

"No."

Stubsen looks at Baer's office. I do, too. The pale yellow concrete's dark now with the light off. I remember interviewing there when Peterson—Sheriff Stan, as they knew him—was still alive and watching the little lines of shadows shake whenever the back of his chair hit the blinds. My interview after, with Baer, was quick. There was probably pressure from the city council, and I'm sure I was the only woman who applied.

"Kara had a picture, didn't she?" Stubsen asks. "From her apartment?"

"And a note."

"Baer said it was taken outside, though."

I look at him this time, keep him talking. "You know her?" I ask. "Kara?"

"Yeah, a little. She was around some when she was younger. When I was just gettin' started."

I nod. "And you took her statement, didn't you, at the hospital?"

Stubsen puffs up a bit. "It woulda been Baer," he says, "but he was off on vacation that weekend. The Bahamas. Stan sent me specifically."

"He must have trusted you." I don't give him a chance to preen. "So do you think Rolenfeld did it?"

Stubsen's eyes dart around the room before landing on Baer's office again. When he looks back at me, he makes a kind of laugh in his throat, almost a grunt, like when he doesn't know what to say and he's been here at my desk for too long. "I guess I dunno," he says after a second.

"Was Dalton ever interviewed?"

"I'm not sure about that. It's not...you know, it's not easy to do that."

"No," I say. "I'm sure it's not."

He reaches over to fiddle with a pen I left out. "I think it's a dead end, anyway. There's no way to know if she's tellin' the truth or not, but Dalton...there's nothin' to go on there."

"Except the picture and the note."

Stubsen looks up. "You think it was somebody, you know, tryin' to scare her or something?"

"Something," I say.

"And you think it's related to what happened back then?"

"The note said that he'd win."

Stubsen's face doesn't change, but he loses a couple inches of height. "Huh," he says. "If it isn't just Kara tryin' to get attention, you know, did you ask her about anything goin' on at work? She's got a big time job, Stan told me. Maybe somebody there has it in for her."

"Sure."

Stubsen claps me on the back. He's been trying this lately, not sure how to touch me.

"Well," he says, "don't waste your time too much."

"No," I tell him, "I won't."


When Stubsen's gone, I open the case file on my computer again, zooming in on the scanned note this time and comparing it to Kara's writing on the form in my desk. I shouldn't have given it to her, but I had no way of knowing what her handwriting looked like otherwise. It happens like that sometimes, that you have to bend some rule just a little if you really want the truth.

Her writing's printed in tall, thin letters like the note. But I'm not an expert at this, and there's only the handful of letters to compare. That writing's hard, deep ridges, while hers was light, but the angle and the way the letters are formed are the same.

I put the note away and read through the case report again. Did she mention a Sebastian then, I wonder, in the hospital when she got the rape kit? She sounded so sure she had, as sure as she was about seeing Dalton grabbing her and holding her down and about it being his voice she heard. It's nowhere in the report, though, and there aren't any leads for a Sebastian. There aren't any leads at all, actually.

I fold her form and drop it into my purse before I shut down my computer for the night.

9

*Kara*

A little after six on Thursday, I watch Brent getting some steaks from Bev's refrigerator and unwrapping their saran covers.

"Just sit," he tells me when I start to get out plates. They're in the same cabinet as always, bargain barn china with the pink flowers around the edges. I wonder how many of these we've shattered on the tile over the years.

"You've gotta be exhausted from cleaning," Brent says.

I tell him his mom's been a help as I take a seat at their dining table. There are still the same three chairs, and I pick the one that was his dad's, facing out towards the deck. But Dalton's smile's here, too, on the front page of the newspaper. He takes up most of the space, standing with his campaign manager under a headline about how he's favored to win the senate seat. A line on a hotbed rezoning issue is just squeezed in at the bottom of the page, like everything after the election's an afterthought.

I look away, out into the woods. "You're staying the week here?" I ask. Brent has his own place in town, a loft over the square that's closer to the factory. But they're spraying it for bugs, so he's here at Bev's for now.

He fiddles with the oven. "Maybe a little longer," he says. "I don't know what day they'll get to my place, and that stuff always gives me a headache. Anyway, the bed in the den's fine, and there's not much traffic on the way to work."

"Good," I say, but I wonder if he's really staying for me. I don't feel scared, exactly, but I know it must be something that's making me hurry through all the piles of things at home. I'm barely even looking at most of the stuff before I throw it into boxes for the donation place out past Felden. There's a stack of bags in the garage now of papers I didn't bother to read.

"Will your mom be home soon?" I ask.

He shakes his head. "At book club."

"Nice," I say. The local book club members are like the cheerleaders in high school, a social circle it's taken Bev years to break into, with Becky, Parker Lange's mom, and Maureen, Dalton's. Until recently, Paige's social circle was carefully stratified with women like Bev, the ones who work, towards the bottom.

"Dalton's going to win, isn't he?" I ask then.

Brent turns away from the plates and looks at me after he's dished out some broccoli from the microwave. He does IT now for Rolenfeld Industries, but he took a class on game theory in college. He's always been into odds, has always known risks. And I know him well enough that he can't bullshit me on this.

"I think he probably will," he says after a beat. "But maybe that's a good thing, right? I mean, then he'll be gone, outta town. He'll be in Washington most of the year, and you won't run into him."

I don't point out that I never run into Dalton in Columbus. I get up and look out the sliding glass door, instead. With the leaves coming down, there are little flashes of the Rolenfeld lake across the woods. In a couple hours, when it's dark, I'll be able to see the light over the dock, a shimmer across the water. I used to think I liked the view, sitting out on my bedroom's balcony reading or watching the light dance across the ripples at night.

"So you think it's just the momentum from his dad's career?" I ask. Because momentum's a big thing here. All these Paige boys turn into their fathers.

Brent makes that grunt he makes when he wants to say something else. "I guess that's it," he says after a second.

"What's he running his campaign on?"

"Honor and honesty. I know. It's a joke. He says in his ads that he *tells it like it is.*"

I squint into the trees. I can't see the corner of my house yet, but I'm sure I'll be able to in a few more weeks. If I'm here in a few more weeks. "Surely everybody sees through him," I say.

Brent shrugs. "Course they do. But everybody here has some connection to him, you know, and that matters more."

When I turn away from the window, Brent's looking at me.

"He's not like you," he says. "Dalton doesn't care that he's full of shit. And he gets away with it."


It's late when I wake up. I'm lying on the bed in the den with an old quilt Bev's mother made tucked around my shoulders. I look at the TV screen, but all I can see is the gray outline of the box and the glowing red button on the DVD player. I must have fallen asleep in the middle of the movie.

It's hard for me to sit up then, to move away from Brent's warmth and slide out from under the quilt. I find my shoes at the foot of the bed and don't know he's awake until he says something.

"Why don't you stay?" he asks, because he's Brent, always making me feel like I could come home if I wanted to.

I think about how easy this would be, first, of how much easier all of this could be. But I tell him I'm awake, that I want to get an early start on some boxes tomorrow.

"You feel okay staying over there by yourself?" he asks.

"Sure. Thanks, though."

He reaches for his phone on the coffee table. "Text me when you get in," he says, like this is much farther, across a city instead of a little woods with the moon high in the sky and just deer and squirrels and raccoons for acres. And crickets, I guess, but those only get me in my sleep.

# 10

*Sam*

Sunday morning, I'm at The Strawberry again, looking up every time the bell over the double glass doors rings and studying everyone who comes in like you do when you know you're missing something.

"Pancakes," Cody says as our waitress walks away. She's another ghost of Paige High, this one from his class. She doesn't even bother to look at me. "You never get pancakes."

"Comfort food," I admit.

"Yeah? Case still bothering you?"

I take a swig of my tea. It has too much honey this morning. Those little blister packets pour out all at once or not at all.

"Unofficially," I remind him.

"Somethin' new come up?"

"Not really." And probably Cody knows better than I do what makes a case in Paige, what should stand out and what shouldn't. The only other mystery I've considered in months involves someone adding a Hitler mustache to one of Dalton Rolenfeld's billboards on the highway out past Dale. Maybe that's why I keep thinking about Kara, because Dalton's face is everywhere.

Cody waits, the way he does, his fingers wrapped all the way around his coffee mug. I check out the tables closest to us. There's a family with two screaming kids in the corner of the old smoking section, but no one's really within earshot.

"Do you think there's ever a good reason not to run DNA on a rape kit?" I ask.

Cody sets down his mug. Some coffee splashes out over the rim.

"She got a rape kit? And they didn't test it?"

I don't confirm this case is *that* case, of course, but he knows it is. I assumed Kara's rape kit was common knowledge, something the whole town must have heard about already, the way they know everything else that's supposed to be confidential.

"I think that's bullshit," he says. "But I can see how it coulda happened."

"Yeah?"

"Well, what would Dalton get, even if she had proof?"

I don't want to answer. Probably no time. Probation, worse case. And that's not taking into account that he's a politician's kid, and wealthy.

"What do *you* think would have happened?" I ask.

"I think he'd smear her to hell," Cody says. "And he'd end up lookin' like the victim. He could smear her way worse than she ever could him. Doesn't matter that she was the one tellin' the truth."

"Even with proof? Even if it came out in court?"

"You think it would?" he counters. "You really think that rape kit wouldn't disappear, or some doctor from somewhere wouldn't come in and say somethin' was wrong with it just because of some shit that had nothin' to do with anything?"

I want to say the system's better than this, but Cody can spot bullshit at least as well as I can. "So you think people around here would buy Dalton's story," I say.

He shrugs. "I think people believe what they wanna believe. And Dalton's family owns this town."

I pick up a piece of toast. I try dunking this one in my tea like Cody does with his coffee, but it still tastes stale to me. Cody's already through his. Maybe it's something about being from here, some good German genes that make hard pumpernickel taste right. I put a glob of the grape jam that's supposed to be local, too, on the next slice, and it at least helps me chew.

I try to change the subject when the rest of our food comes, a plate of pancakes I'll have to push most of on Cody and his usual breakfast with Canadian bacon and eggs and steaming hash browns that smell like canola oil. I ask him about some recent renovation projects he's been doing, but he brings the conversation back to Kara as soon as the waitress disappears again.

"It musta been bad," he says. "I think she dropped outta law school because of it."

"All rapes are bad." It's out before I can think. So I hurry to say something else. "How well do you know Nate Stubsen?"

Cody's eyebrows do their bunching thing. I wonder sometimes if he knows he's doing it, if maybe he used it back in the day to make all the cheerleaders swoon over him the way they still seem to.

"Stubsen?" he asks. "Why?"

"I think he's hitting on me." This is true, at least.

"Yeah? You interested?"

A dry bite of pancake sticks in my throat. Sometimes I forget Cody hasn't known me that long. And he never assumes anything.

"No." I take a sip of tea. "I don't think we'd be a good fit."

Cody nods. "I don't know him real well. Heard he was a good tight end. Played basketball, too, but he was a ways ahead of me."

"How much older?"

"Eight or nine years maybe. I think he went right into the force. I remember seeing him drivin' a patrol car around town when I was just in middle school."

Through the rest of our conversation, I can't stop thinking about Stubsen and how much 'Stubsen' sounds like 'Sebastian' when Cody says it. My pancakes are sitting like lead in my stomach by the time Cody pays—again, before I can even catch the waitress's eye—and is holding open the door to the parking lot.

"There wasn't anybody *with* Dalton, you don't think?" he asks once we're outside. "Somebody else here that Kara needs to be worried about?"

I start to tell him I can't speculate about this, then ask why he thought of it. I haven't told him anything about Dalton talking to someone else in that room.

Cody looks at the street. "I don't know if it's true," he says.

"That Dalton's gay?"

Cody's head whips back to me.

"It doesn't matter," I tell him. "Rape's about control, not desire. About hurting someone because you can."

He's frowning when we get to his truck. "And it couldn't have been a threesome or somethin'? That Dalton had planned, I mean, when he found her?"

It stops me. 'Threesome' isn't a word I expected to come out of Cody's mouth. There's something almost Southern about him, too proper for that. Like Sheriff Stan, actually, now that I think about it, but I never got the feeling Peterson's drawl was that real.

"I don't know," I admit, and then I can't get it out of my head for the rest of the day.

# 11



*Kara*

Nancy Keller's salon is bustling at nine Monday morning even though I'm her first appointment. Her front parlor's obviously still the feminine hub of Paige, delivery people dropping by with bits of news from the weekend and women coming in with their lattes from the coffee place on the square to gossip in front of the big picture window that looks out at Third Avenue.

This is how it's been since I can remember, even before my mom passed away and before I understood what most of the talking was about. There's still pink glass at the edges of the mirrors and old dryer hoods in the corner. Nancy hasn't changed, either; her perfect rows of ringlets are the same bright chestnut they've been forever.

She's just started to use the razor to angle the hair around my face—that's how they're wearin' 'em, she says, in the city—and smiles at me in the mirror as she regales my big city lawyerly accomplishments for the benefit of the women loitering out front.

"Not quite a lawyer," I remind her. "I didn't graduate, that year."

She looks down, studying a section of my hair she's cut about five times now. "A consultant, isn't it?"

"For taxes."

"'s the same thing. You made somethin' of it, anyway. And Bev says you can work from home most a the time now. Suits you just right, if you ask me. A girl your age needs some freedom."

I smile. That's just how Bev would have put it, the pep talk she probably gave me at the time. She took over saying all these things when my mom died.

Nancy's eyes dart to the front window then, to Maureen Rolenfeld walking past on the sidewalk. It feels like I'm frozen for a second, but just about anything can do this to me now, can pause everything else happening around me and make me forget to breathe, to talk, to function like I'm trying to show people here that I can.

"You're doin' great," Nancy tells me under her breath.

I nod and try to return her smile in the mirror, because of course this is more than a haircut; this is like a coming out in Paige society again. I can feel the others' eyes on me once Maureen's gone. I look down and flick some pieces of hair off my cape. You'd think you could start over as someone new, if you're away for long enough, but this town's memory is long and perfect. So you start with whatever scandal you left, right in the middle of it again.

"So you seein' anybody?" Nancy asks.

"Not right now," I tell her, like I haven't spent the last decade thinking I'll never see anyone again. It was just like a haircut, really, one of the parts of who I used to be that was snipped away that night and made it harder to recognize myself afterwards.

"Plenty a time," Nancy says. "You're still young."

When she's finished cutting, she says she wants to use the curler in the back. I tell her as I follow that I don't need this today, that I'm just doing more work around the house and won't see anyone, but she ignores me.

"What about the humane society thing?" she asks as she wraps the first section of my hair around a big-barreled curling iron. "Have you thought about if you'll go?"

"I don't know if I have a dress."

Nancy bends around the corner to look out at the front room. "You've got nothin' to be ashamed of," she says. "You wouldn't believe how many people this kinda thing happens to. I don't think you know my daughter-in-law, Shelby? Same thing happened to her up at school. And people were nasty about it, same as with you."

"I'm sorry," I say automatically. Because that's what we always are for these things, sorry. There's never any talk of catching them ahead of time, of doing something to stop them from happening.

Nancy nods. "You just keep your head up, honey," she says. "And know your mom and your daddy would be so proud a you."

*　　*

Tuesday night, Brent's sitting on the edge of my bed eating his usual German sausage pizza from The Slice as I try on dresses for the gala.

I'd forgotten I left all my formal clothes here. I used to think I could just come back anytime I might need a dress or some heels. But as I rifle through the old wire hangers, all the dresses strike me as so young, so not *me* anymore.

The first one I try's a simple black sheath that skims over my belly and hits at the knee. It's one I could have worn to work, I think, with a jacket. I don't know why I didn't take it to Columbus with me.

"What's that?" Brent asks when I come out of the closet. "Is that your funeral dress?"

I laugh. That must be why I left it here. Funerals are like state events in Paige. Everyone who's home goes. It doesn't matter if you knew the person or not.

I roll my eyes at Brent's face and go put on the next, a gray jersey v-neck with long sleeves and ruching over the waist. I'm surprised it still fits, that my body hasn't changed more.

Brent closes the pizza box when I come out. "Nice," he says. "You really wore that when you were young, huh?"

I stick out my tongue. They say you go one way or the other afterwards, either covering everything or covering nothing. I don't know which direction I went. Maybe I didn't change enough, and that's why I still feel this way sometimes.

"I really think a pantsuit would be okay," I tell him.

Brent shakes his head. "All the girls'll be in dresses, and you look good. Wear something sexy and snub your nose at all of 'em."

I make a joke of this and come out next in a black bandage

dress that looks like it belongs on someone a foot shorter and a decade younger than I am. This dress should be out careening around fraternity parties like I never did.

Brent whistles. "That one," he says. "Definitely that."

"I was kidding."

He waggles his eyebrows to make me laugh. "I wasn't."

I change into a simple mock neck sheath next.

"Come on," he says when I come back out. "You looked great in that other one. Kym Hartmann would hate you with the power of a thousand suns if you showed up to the gala in that."

"And that's what we're going for? Kym Hartmann hating me?"

"That's *exactly* what we're going for," he says. "You need a little self-esteem boost."

I turn around to study the back of the sheath in the mirror. It's a little loose over my hips and falls just past my knees. "Have you asked Kym? To go with you, I mean."

"Are you kidding?"

I glance over my shoulder at him. "It's not working out?" I ask.

He's looking at his phone now. "No. I mean, I don't know. I don't think we're gonna be a thing. Leah's been driving her nuts flirting with me all the time, and she's pretty pissed. And anyway, I'm going with *you*."

I leave on the mock neck and bend to go through some shoes, digging around under my old shower flip flops for a pair of closed-toe slides I wore during undergrad. I think they'd still fit if it weren't for my bunions. "You really don't think I could wear a pantsuit?" I ask.

"I think you could pull off whatever you wanted," Brent says, and actually this time he sounds like he means it. He must think I'm pretty damaged now, to need this.

"Uh huh."

"I'm glad you're going, is what I mean. It's a good statement. And your dad would like it."

I mumble something to agree as I pull out some kitten heels.

"Nice," he says when I try them on, but he's looking at his phone again. Then he looks at the clock on my nightstand.

"You should get home," I tell him. "You have work in the morning."

"No. It isn't that." He slumps into the pillows at my headboard and looks out the window. "I've been thinking about something and wasn't sure if I should bring it up."

When he doesn't go on, I sit down on the edge of the bed. My left heel strap slides off the back of my ankle.

"You're feeling all right, aren't you?" he asks after a second. "Safe, I mean, and not, like, obsessing or remembering or anything?"

I wait. I'm not sure what obsessing is, exactly, over something like this. And I've always remembered.

Brent leans back and looks at me. "It's Sebastian," he says. "I know that's what you heard, but I've been thinking about it, and could it have been *Stubsen*, instead, that Dalton was talking to, as in Nate Stubsen?"

"Stubsen?"

"It's just the name, and that I think they know each other pretty well, he and Dalton. You remember him, don't you? The cop?"

I try to picture Stubsen's face always towering over everyone else's at the station. "You think he was at the party?" I ask.

Brent shrugs. "It's just the only name that sounds right to me."

"I didn't really know him, though. We never talked or anything."

"So?"

"Well, if he didn't know me..."

We sit in the quiet for a while, thinking about this.

"You've always assumed this was personal, haven't you?" Brent asks after a few minutes. "But what if it wasn't? I mean, there's no reason to think it was, is there?"

"No," I say, standing and fixing the strap on my heel. "I guess not."

# 12

*August, twelve years earlier*

Dalton Rolenfeld hosted his high school class's five year reunion. Those were common in places like Paige, where the college kids like to come home and settle down around that time. Nobody in rural Ohio waits to couple off until their ten year.

You could see all the lights in the Rolenfeld mansion from the street, but behind it, the lake was a shadow, the moon just a sliver overhead. The humidity hadn't broken yet that year, and night was the time for skinny-dipping, for drunken hoots and shrieks and splashes that seemed to come out of nowhere.

Kara Peterson, a couple days before she'd head back to the city to start her second year of law school, wasn't a friend of Dalton's, exactly, even though they were neighbors. They'd always run in different circles.

She was a little ways away from the others, treading water off the far bank, when he joined her. She'd gotten in on her side of the lake, where she could change out of her clothes in the darkness, and she didn't know anyone was close by until she felt his leg wrap around hers under the water.

They were near enough to the others to hear voices and catch a splash every now and then, so they didn't say anything. His arm came around her waist, and she floated back into him.

They stayed suspended there listening to the party until Brent called her name. Then Dalton disappeared under the water.

# 13

*Sam*

Wednesday morning, I glance at the hallway to make sure no one's coming before I play the video on my computer again. It's just twenty minutes of security footage, the ten minutes before and after Kara's rape.

I watch it all the way through this time. The night vision makes the picture black and white, shades of gray tinged with green, but I can see the whole sweep of the Rolenfelds' front lawn—a few cars that come and go around the drive, a bunch of faces, and a bare tree in the middle of the screen that catches the light. Dalton's standing under one of the outdoor floods just a couple yards away from the camera like it's a spotlight. He turns the camera's way every now and then like he's playing to it, like he knows someone will watch this.

People circle around him a few times, but he doesn't move. Right in the middle of the clip, he's making out with some girl whose name is noted in the report—Parker Lange, I think, the dentist's daughter.

The feed never cuts out, and it doesn't look like it was altered in any way. That was enough to clear him of the accusation, apparently, since Kara remembered the numbers on the nightstand clock, 11:10. The Rolenfelds didn't offer footage of the rest of that night, and there wasn't a warrant to get it, so it would have been lost years ago. That's how those systems work, holding footage for two or three days and then taping over it with new.

No one thought about whether the clock in that room had been changed for daylight savings or if there was a power outage and it might have gone out randomly in the middle of some stormy night. No one thought about anything, it seems like, after the footage got to the station. And that was really just a formality.

I watch the video again, then *x* out of the screen when I see Stubsen's patrol car pulling in.

# 14

*Kara*

Wednesday night, I stay up working on my laptop, going through client files online and getting everything ready for the end of the year like this isn't just October. It's a good change from stuffing bags, at least, from trying to sort the remnants of my old life into piles.

I'm getting ready for bed a little past eleven when I hear the scratching—soft, at first, like the scrape of a branch against a window.

When it happens again, I creep over to my curtains and peek between them like something might actually be outside, but it's a new moon tonight, too dark to see anything.

I wait and listen for it again, like it might be part of a pattern. Like crickets are, or bullfrogs, the way you get to know what's coming. I can feel my heartbeat in my temples when I finally sit down at the foot of the bed and pick up my cell phone.

*Are you up?* I text Brent.

He calls right away. I jump when the phone lights up in my

hand.

"You okay?" he asks.

I look at the curtains. "You're awake," I say. But of course he is; this is when he's usually at his computer gaming or whatever he does so late that should make me feel better, knowing he's right next door, his window looking out over the drive. I hold the phone to my ear as I go to the living room and switch on the outside lights.

"I'll come over," Brent says, because he can hear something isn't right in my voice, the way he can always hear these things.

"It's okay," I tell him, squinting out into the glow of the floodlights. There's no one there, of course, and these woods are full of raccoons and squirrels and possums always rustling around in the leaves or digging in the trash cans. I remember one fat raccoon who used to scamper across the roof and look down through the skylight with his yellow eyes. I look up. The skylights are dark tonight, reflecting the sofa and the kitchen island.

"What was it?" Brent asks.

"Scratching."

"Not knocking? Like before?" Like pipes, he means, in old houses like this one. I used to hear knocking sometimes when I was little, when I was still scared of houses and not of people.

"No. It must have just been a branch or something."

"You're sleeping upstairs? So no one can see in?"

"That's a good idea." But no one's ever been looking into my windows before. It's just these woods, something about them, and something about me now, too, I guess, that can do this to me.

"I'll come over," Brent says, and I don't stop him.

*     *

Thursday, I start to run out of the little pyrex containers of food Bev's filled my fridge with, so I make a trip to Gleson's grocery in town. As I drive up Clay Street, I think of how different Paige looks in the daytime and with everyone milling around the sidewalks on the square in their sweater vests and Patagonia jackets. Gleson's parking lot's mostly empty, but the smell of those cinnamon spice pinecones that always give me a headache wafts out through the automatic doors.

Inside, everything's the same as I remember, the same bright blue signs over the aisles and the cashiers and bag boys flirting over the checkout lanes. There's a wooden box of pumpkins and gourds by the produce section and a poster for straw bales out back.

"Kara?"

I turn away from some wrinkly apples in time to see Parker Lange just before she hugs me. She still smells like that perfume from Victoria's Secret she wore in high school.

"Sweetie," she says, her cheerleader's high blonde pony whipping around her cheeks as she shakes her head. "I can't believe I'm seein' your face here."

I try to laugh, because I guess I can't believe my face is here, either. I knew hers would be, though.

"How long are you in town?" she asks. "We outta get some lunch, catch up."

"Not long," I tell her, and agree, because we won't really do this. Parker and I have never gotten together. We don't have anything to catch up on.

"You'll be at the humane society shindig, though," she says.

"Right. Of course."

She grins. She's gotten veneers since I've seen her last, a blinding blue-white that look like chiclets across the front of her smile. "You're not gonna make trouble for me now, are you?" Of course she says this like she knows I couldn't, even if I tried.

I don't know what to say. So I don't try.

Then she laughs, drawing some more attention, and waves a hand in front of her face. A bunch of silver bracelets clang together on her wrist. "You know me and Dalton are together again, don't you?" she asks.

"I didn't." They were together in high school, the homecoming king and queen. I didn't think Dalton had dated since then.

Her smile doesn't move. "And don't think I don't remember *you* dancing with him at senior prom, how you stole that last dance from me."

"Prom," I say. "I barely remember."

Parker purses her lips. "But don't worry," she tells me, "*I've forgiven you.*"

I open my mouth, but nothing comes out. Parker's all church like her mom, that special religion that lives to perch in a string bikini in the dunking booth at the St. Mark's fish fry.

She makes Paige small talk for a couple more minutes, waving over my shoulder at a few people who pass by. I try to keep my face in this smile that's starting to hurt my cheeks, because we both know we're putting on a show here.

Parker gives me another hug before she goes, when Mrs. Markel's waving at us, and her perfume sticks in my nose for the rest of the day.

# 15



*Sam*

Friday over my lunch break, I meet up with Kara Peterson at The Strawberry. The place is quiet today, and the waitresses are different, I think, more friendly during the week. But maybe it's just because I'm not with Cody this time.

I order my tea and a little lunch—a turkey sandwich like the one I usually take with me to the station, this one made with meat from the processing plant out by Dale. Kara just has coffee.

I study her from across the booth as she fiddles with something in her purse, but I can't see any difference in her today than the first time I met her. Her hair's pulled back in the same sleek pony, and there's foundation carefully dotted under her eyes and around her nose. She's a little anxious maybe, but that's expected; she doesn't know why I've asked to meet with her, and I can't pull off the "new to town, just seeking friendship" act for very long.

I ask her about some places to eat that I already know about, then about where to go to get an oil change.

"Do you know the Flecks?" she asks. "They have a shop just out past the junction."

I thank her, and she takes another sip of coffee, both hands wrapped around one of the cream-colored mugs they say were handmade years ago at some shop on the square but that look just like the ones from IHOP back home.

"You're feeling okay at the house?" I ask, not working it in like I wanted, however you work a rape into a friendly lunch. "I mean, you're settling in okay? It must be tough to come home after being away so long."

Kara nods. "It is, a little. I've gotten used to things in the city. Like you probably did, right? Groceries, you know, and..." Her voice trails off.

"Right. I could really go for some Indian food about now."

She smiles and tells me about the place with Ohio's best gulab jamun that's just a few blocks from her apartment in Columbus. "I swear I'm losing honey weight," she says, "just being away from it."

"But you feel safe here."

She looks back at her coffee. "I've always felt safe here," she says.

"Of course." I take another sip of my tea and try to think of what to ask her next, what it is I'm really looking for.

"You can ask me," she says then, as soon as the table next to ours is finished being bussed and we're out of earshot again. "Whatever it is. I didn't it make up to get in Dalton's way or anything. I don't care about the election."

"No," I say, automatically. "I know." And I think I *do* know this.

She waits, watching me from across the table.

"It's about the time," I tell her once a family's been seated a few booths down from us and are flipping noisily through their menus. "You were sure those were the numbers you saw on the clock, 11:10?"

"Right." Her face doesn't change. She's stuck to this story. She must have believed it to not just have given something vague, a longer timeframe that would have made it harder for Dalton to alibi out. She was the sheriff's daughter; she would have known better, I think, if she'd been lying.

"Is there something new?" she asks when I don't say anything right away.

I wrestle with a blister packet and drop some more honey into my tea. "No, unfortunately. And if this, if talking about it stirs up too much..."

She shakes her head. "I don't mind. I know it was Dalton. I just want to understand the things I don't yet. It's hard to get past it, you know, until you understand."

"Of course." So I start on my other questions. "Do you remember how you got upstairs?"

"I went up to go to the bathroom. There was someone in the powder room on the main floor."

"And no idea why you were in a guest room, why you ended up in there instead of in Dalton's room?"

"Not really." She's holding her coffee mug again. It's empty.

"He grabbed you, though," I say. "You remember that. Where?"

"Inside the room."

"Not in the hallway?"

"No. Inside the room."

"You're sure."

She waits. She's been sure of everything.

I glance out the window, at a truck stopped at the light. "And I don't mean to offend you, but I have to ask, because it could affect some other details. The report said you hadn't been drinking."

"No," she says.

"No," I echo, and then I try to change the subject and pretend I'm not still thinking about this.

*     *

My weekend goes quickly, and Monday morning, I'm just getting into the office as Stubsen's mixing some kind of protein powder into his coffee, his usual routine. He beelines for my desk as soon as I sit down, then makes small talk as I start up my computer.

"No big parties or anything, then, huh?" he asks, about the weekend.

"Not even one."

"But you'll be at the humane society thing this Saturday."

"That's right. Cody Muller's taking me." This isn't a lie, really.

Stubsen freezes for a second, his eyes flicking away, then back to me. "Great," he says. "That's great. You know they got a big check from the Rolenfelds to redo the place. They'll be gettin' new pens for the dogs and everything."

I sit back in my chair. "Does that happen every year?" I ask. "Or just because of the election?"

Stubsen grins. "Maybe that. I don't think they've told anybody yet, though, so don't go spreadin' it around."

He waits while I click into my weekly schedule. I have it memorized; things don't change much around here.

"Are you still lookin' into that case?" he asks then. "The one with Kara Peterson?" I can smell his aftershave when he leans closer. It's stronger this morning, or maybe I've just lost the tolerance to it I build up through the weeks.

"Not really." He can't know I'm still accessing Kara's file. I downloaded it and keep it in a folder on my home screen with a bunch of paperwork so no one can see how often I'm opening it. Sometimes transparency can get in the way.

Stubsen looks around the office. We're the first ones here, and the lights in the hallway clicked back off a few minutes after I got in. "Anyway," he says, "you can ask me about it, you know. I talked to all the witnesses afterwards. Stan had me follow up personally."

"There were witnesses?" The file didn't say anything about witnesses, about any followup.

He shakes his head. "Not like that. Nobody saw anything."

Fifty people, at least, in one house, and no one saw anything. "You don't believe her," I say.

Stubsen shrugs. "Well, one of 'em said she'd been drinkin'. And that maybe she'd had a thing for Dalton and he wasn't into her back. Like I said, all the girls here do."

My fingers curl over the keyboard, and I set my hands on my lap. That's what the defense always says, that the woman *liked* the man, or at least that she'd been interested. And how can you trust someone who was interested in a rapist?

"Does that mean she wasn't raped?" I ask, and say "sorry" right after. "I have a headache," I tell him.

Stubsen shrugs this off. "It's Monday. You need some real stuff," he says, lifting his coffee mug. "Not that tea."

"That's it. Maybe I'll try yours sometime. So who was it?"

"Who?"

"The witness."

"Don't remember. Some of the other kids, though. One was talkin' to her downstairs just before it happened. Supposedly happened."

"Not kids," I say, automatically. She was 24.

Stubsen frowns at me. "Right," he says. "Yeah."

I look at my computer screen and count to three. People like Stubsen become predictable, if you give them the chance.

"I've been meanin' to say somethin' to you about it, actually," he says, right on the next beat.

I angle my chair to him like I'm listening.

"It's that it wouldn't matter if I believed her, so much." He shifts closer on my desk, leaning in. "There've been...things with the Rolenfelds. You know, small town, lots a money. There were two ladies at the factory who filed charges against Bob for harassment a while back, and they dropped 'em, and then there was this thing in the city we got wind of back here. Just talk, I mean."

"What was it?"

"Some kinda assault."

"But just talk?"

Stubsen nods. "It's that, you know...and I wouldn't say this here."

"No," I say, and lean forward, because I can keep secrets, too. Every town has a few.

He glances over my shoulder at Baer's dark office. "It's that I think Rolenfeld probably has a lot of friends here still. You know..."

"Yeah," I say. "I get it."

The hallway lights come back on. Stubsen nods and slides off my desk. "But if you need any help, or if ever you wanna talk about it, just ask me."

I thank him and don't open Kara's folder again until he's left for patrol.

# 16

*December 20, ten years ago*

Dalton Rolenfeld went upstairs a few minutes before Kara. He was waiting on the balcony, a hallway lined with a bunch of carved mahogany the maid could never get all the dust out of.

Kara stood in the foyer until some others who were getting drinks to take down to the basement had gone back. Rock music was playing on the speakers there, a constant bass that buzzed up through the cherry floors.

She downed the rest of her drink, took a deep breath, and met Dalton on the landing.

# 17

*Kara*

I wake up out of air, my legs tangled in the sheets.

It takes a while to see where I am, for the shadows to swirl around me and turn into things again—the dresser on the far wall, the curtains over the windows with a sliver of moonlight barely peeking through, the posts overhead that used to hold the gauzy white canopy my mom got from one of her magazines.

There's one of those frosted plug-in nightlights in the bathroom that sends some light out under the door, and I stumble towards it. My legs are slow, not bending right. It can feel like being paralyzed at the beginning. But my therapist said that's normal. I must have been kicking hard in my sleep.

I gag over the toilet, but nothing comes up. When I sit back on my ankles, I smell peaches, the lotion I was wearing that night, from the bottle I got from Bev in my Christmas stocking the year before. Phantom scents are normal, too, though, when your brain's stuck in some other time. At least I'm not still in my old bedroom, I think, that I came upstairs to Dad's like Brent suggested. It would probably have been worse if I'd woken up where I did that morning.

The gagging doesn't last long this time, and when I stand and look at myself in the mirror, I look like I did for the year or so after it happened, in my first floor apartment in the city where it didn't matter that no one was ever on the other side of the windows.

My legs are still shaky, so I sit down on the toilet lid, counting things I can see and feel and smell. The peaches are still overwhelming in my nose, but I can count tiles on the floor, can see the window and the sink and the towels. I can hear the heat kicking on and the wind whistling through the trees outside and my breath still coming fast.

My skin's clammy, and there are red patches over my wrists. They say trauma's an adrenal thing, something chemical that has to leave the body somehow, to work its way out through your pores or your kidneys like a poison that clings to your tissues. I guess it makes sense that mine comes through my skin, where anyone can see it. I run a washcloth under some cool water and hold it over the side of my face.

My cheeks have warmed the towel and I'm walking back to the bed, past the big floral armchair that my mom reupholstered the year before she died, when I hear the knock.

My phone's lit up on the nightstand, and I go for it before I open the door to the bedroom, like I might call someone, like there really could be something out there that's worse than what's in here.

The phone shows a notification for a missed text and two missed calls from Brent.

I rush down the stairs, and of course it's him at the front door.

He grabs me by the shoulders as soon as I unlock it, pushing me back inside.

"You're okay," he says, like maybe he can know this.

I open my mouth. He keeps walking us back towards the living room, and we fall down onto the sofa when we get there.

"I thought I heard you scream," he says. "I looked outside, and you had all these lights on."

That's when I see them, too—not just the ones over the kitchen island, but the overheads all through the living room and both outdoor floods, too.

I start to tell him I didn't do this. I don't remember hitting the lights on my way to the door. I couldn't have gotten to the outside ones without walking out of my way, all the way across the living room to my old bedroom. But I can't say this out loud.

I look around and try to remember the steps I took. That's how you do it, they say, how you identify the times you've blocked away. You look for minutes that are missing. Like the calls I didn't hear. When nothing comes back to me, I tell myself I must have just been sleepwalking like I used to when I was stressed. That's what I told people it was, anyway, stress. That's why I said I dropped out of law school, too.

Brent scoots closer on the sofa and wraps his arms around me. I can feel his heart in his hands now—slow, steady like always. We're backwards here; we're usually sitting the other way around.

Maybe that's why this feels wrong, with him on my right.

"You're okay," he tells me, then, "this isn't your fault."

I don't move. I look out through the living room windows and focus on the white maple outside. My mom's empty bird feeder that always fed the squirrels, instead, is swinging around in the wind.

"This isn't your fault," Brent repeats.

I nod and sit back into him. That's what both of my therapists said, too. But what if it *is* my fault? What if this is something I did to myself?

# 18




*Sam*


I don't expect to see Kara Peterson as I'm finishing my first tea Tuesday morning. She walks right in from the hallway—like she's used to doing, I guess, or at least like she used to—and comes straight to me.

I try not to let my face show surprise when she gets to my desk, but you always are, with cases like hers. They're all a little more complicated than the reports make them sound.

"Can I talk to you?" she asks. She's not wearing concealer today, and I can see dark bags under her eyes. Her hair's in a bushy ponytail, not straightened like before.

"Of course," I say, and then something about the warm weather recently—a bit of an Indian summer, the guy on the weather channel said—as I lead her to the little room that works like an interrogation room, the office with the crooked blinds where I met her the first time. Kara's already turned around to face me when I close the door.

"I lied to you," she says.

"Okay. Can I get you something? Coffee?"

She shakes her head and sits down, gripping the edge of the table with her hands like it might come after her, too.

When she looks out the window, so do I. I don't know what either of us are expecting to see out there.

"I didn't go upstairs to go to the bathroom that night. I went upstairs to meet Dalton Rolenfeld by one of the bedrooms."

I give her a minute. We listen to a truck chugging down 31 and past the ice cream place on the corner, where there's always a line of cars waiting to get out of the movie theater when I'm driving home.

"You and Dalton had a relationship?" I ask.

Kara shakes her head. She's still looking out the window. "Not a relationship," she says. "But that's why I went there. We'd had...I guess I thought that we might."

"That doesn't make this your fault."

She lets out a little noise like a laugh, but of course nothing about these cases is ever funny. Then she looks at me, holds eye contact. "I could see his face in the bedroom, like I told you—that was true—but I followed him in. It was Dalton who grabbed me as soon as I got inside."

"The light was on?"

"No. The door was open behind me. I could see him."

"And then it was dark."

"Right," she says. "But he didn't let go of me."

"Did you see him hit the lights? Or close the door?"

She shakes her head. So we wait there for a minute, both of us looking out the window again, her sitting now, me standing on the other side of the desk.

"So this *was* something personal," I say, when probably I shouldn't.

"I don't know. I thought so."

"Do you remember anything else?"

She looks like she's going to say something. So I give her the time.

"I lied about not having anything to drink," she says after a few seconds.

"You were drinking."

She has my eyes again, trying to show me she's telling the truth. "I'd heard about cases like this before," she says, "when the woman admitted she was drinking, and I knew even back at the hospital that no one would believe me about what happened if I told them I'd had something to drink."

I don't know how to respond to this. She's right.

"It was just one drink I had, though. I never had more than one. Just a beer."

"In a can?"

"A cup." She looks down at the table. "I wasn't drunk. And I don't think my drink was spiked, either. I remember everything."

"I know," I say, and mean it. These aren't things victims ever get wrong; even when there are times that are missing, they still know everything that happened in the times they remember.

I sit down, and we're quiet for a couple minutes as I write some notes in a mini yellow pad I'll keep in my desk for the rest of the day and then take home with me. This doesn't belong in her file. It doesn't change what happened, and it could only be used against her.

Kara's fidgeting with her hands, peeling at a cuticle when I look back up at her.

"There's something else," I say.

She looks at the window again. There are just a few cars out on 31 now. Traffic won't pick up until lunchtime. "I'm not really sure," she says. "And you'll think...I know it sounds crazy."

"That's okay."

"I heard crickets."

It takes me a beat to respond. "Crickets?" I ask.

She nods. "That's one of the things I remembered when I had a nightmare right before I came home. But I was thinking about them, the noises, during..." Her face is red now, blotchy.

I've seen this before. You can only hold these things inside for so long. "Let me get you a coffee," I say.

She shakes her head. "No. I know it was December. But they were so clear."

"You're sure it was crickets? And not something that sounded the same? Like a...a bed creaking, or a door?"

"I'm sure." She wipes an eye with a sleeve. She doesn't carry tissues in her purse. "I know it sounds crazy. But I felt like I had to say something now."

I let the *now* go, because this timeline that starts now isn't something either of us understand yet. But I know there's a timeline. There always is when these things come back up.

"The note," I say. "Do you think that was..."

"Dalton." She sounds just as sure as she's sounded about everything else.

I set the notepad down on the table and wish I didn't believe her.

# 19


*Kara*


Brent comes over Tuesday night with dinner from the new Mexican place downtown. It's not as good as Paco's, but it's faster in the traffic when the factory lets out. We eat at the table tonight, but with the plastic forks and knives that came in the bag, sawing and scraping and stabbing little holes in the styrofoam containers.

"So what'd you tell the cop?" he asks once he's finished a rant about some new HR training at his work, a program Kym Hartmann's running.

"That I'd had a beer." I don't mention following Dalton, meeting him at the top of the stairs, because Brent wouldn't understand. I want to say I've kept this from him because he's always hated Dalton and would judge me for it, but that's probably not the whole reason.

He pushes his box away. He's been finished for a while. I still have half an enchilada left.

"But you'd had more than that," he says.

"No."

"I remember you taking a shot. You remember, don't you, they had 'em on the pool table?"

I try to remember the pool table. Nothing comes. "In the basement?" I ask.

Brent looks at my food, then at me. "Maybe you don't remember," he says after a minute, and reaches across the table for my hand.

"I wasn't taking shots. I never took shots."

He's looking at my hand, stroking it with his thumb when he finally responds. "Kara, you, uh...you did that night."

I almost pull away. "No."

He shakes his head. "It's okay," he says. "You probably forgot a lot because of...well, what happened. That's normal afterwards, isn't it?"

That's when I get up, leave my food and go to my dad's old chair. I sit down. But it feels different, wrong, looking over at the sofa where we usually sit.

Brent comes and stands by the ottoman. "I'm not saying you were drunk or anything. I'm not saying you don't remember the important..."

"Where was the pool table? That night."

He looks behind him at the windows, at the maple lit up by the floodlight. "In the main room downstairs, with everybody else. Where it always was."

"No."

Brent looks back at me. "I don't think you should worry about it. This is something that can happen, isn't it?"

"Disassociation," I say.

He's shaking his head, but he doesn't contradict me. "You

didn't say anything to the cop about the crickets, though?"

I think about this for just a second before I tell him that I didn't.

He sits down on the ottoman. "Well," he says, "that's probably for the best. I don't think she'd have taken you seriously if you had."

My mind pulls away from this as the night goes on, drifts to all the dresses for the humane society gala that don't look right on me anymore and all the bags of things I don't know what to do with out in the garage. I've almost stopped thinking about crickets and the shots I don't remember taking when Brent asks if I'm up for a movie.

He's on the sofa with me now, his knees running into mine like we don't really fit here anymore. We've been watching TV for a while, sinking down into these old cushions and looking out the back windows whenever the wind blows the branches around or some leaves tumble across the light.

Brent shifts, turns to me. "There's something else on your mind," he says. "Something's bothering you."

"I don't remember getting home," I tell him after a minute of us sitting like this.

"What?"

"Afterwards. The first thing I remember is waking up the next morning. Everything in between, it's...gone."

Brent shakes his head like maybe he doesn't believe me. But that's not right. Brent's always believed me. This feeling's just my defenses turning up, I guess, just the way I am in Paige now. Sometimes it feels like the hills around this town are walls, and I only need to get through them, to be anywhere else and I'd turn back into *someone* else, into someone who sleeps and remembers and doesn't hear things. Someone who doesn't feel like they need to lie.

"Well, you had to have walked, right?" Brent asks. "I mean, you wouldn't have driven right next door."

I don't say anything, because of course I don't remember.

"You still had your clothes on?"

I nod. But I couldn't find my underwear that morning. I wasn't wearing any under my jeans. That should have struck me as wrong, I think now. I should have said something at the hospital. But I don't say this now, even to Brent.

"So you must have gotten dressed, after…"

I stand up. "I think I'm just tired," I tell him. "I should go to bed."

He stands and goes to the basket where we keep the blankets for the sofa.

I turn away when I feel the tears pushing up behind my eyes. It's like there's too much pressure in my head today. But there's something else with my body, too, a feeling like I really might run away. Like I won't be able to stop it. I don't know how to tell Brent this. He'll think I'm crazy, too, if he sees it.

So I let him go home, telling him I'm fine over and over like saying it enough times will make it true.

"You're sure you don't want me to stay?" he asks a few minutes later, when he has his coat on and is standing by the kitchen door.

"I'm sure," I say, and lock the door behind him.


Later, with hot water burning my cheeks and the upstairs bathroom full of steam, I try to remember the pool table. It's not that I don't want to remember it. I've said all along that I wanted to remember, that I wanted to know whatever I was missing, even though my therapist told me that's not always for the best.

When I dry off with one of Dad's old towels, I open the medicine cabinet. I used to take a Benadryl with a glass of wine on nights that felt like this one. But that's all, one glass of wine; I haven't had a beer since that night. I've never liked shots.

I find the Benadryl behind some Sudafed and Motrin. It's barely expired, and I take a couple gel caps before I pull on my pajamas and crawl into bed.

# 20



*Sebastian*

I see her shadow sometimes when she passes by the window. I can always tell when she's fallen asleep with the light on and when she's still up. She moves around so much. It's like she can't help it.

Tonight, she's sleeping like there isn't any reason she shouldn't rest easy.

# 21



*Kara*


I spend the next days focused on the house, sorting what's left into piles and then stuffing them into bags to donate like that woman on the house show Bev watches does. Nothing here sparks joy.

I leave the TV on for noise and only turn it off when Brent comes over in the evenings, when I tell him over and over that I'm okay. I don't look it, I guess, or he wouldn't be here with takeout from a different place each night. It's like he knows there's more in me still, more memories stuck somewhere in my brain, and we're just waiting for the next one to break loose.

Saturday night before the gala, Brent's sitting on my old mattress while I do my makeup in that bathroom. I don't know where the matching towels went, but it has the same seashell tiles my mom helped me pick out when I was seven, the same pedestal sink and big, round lights I used to think were like the ones in Broadway dressing rooms.

They should make me look better now, but the circles under

my eyes seem to pop under them. Maybe Dad replaced the bulbs wrong, with daylight instead of warm. I remember how the kitchen and the living room ended up with funny cold pockets a couple years after Mom died, when he bought the bulbs himself. We can look so different when you change the light.

I put on another coat of concealer, but it's not a match for my skin anymore. I don't know if it's too dark or too olive. But maybe this is just the light, too; it's been my shade since high school.

I haven't really slept a full night since the Benadryl Tuesday, and I woke up Wednesday morning with a headache. That was just from my brain looking for things, though, turning creaks and pipe knocks and wind in the trees into something else. Nothing's ever outside when I get up and turn on the lights.

It's been a long time since I've worn mascara, and the tube I packed's mostly dried out. At least my hair doesn't give me away, I think. I curled it with my mom's old thin-barreled iron, so the waves should hold for a couple hours now the humidity's gone down.

Brent sits up and whistles when I come out, and I make a little twirl in front of the bed.

"You look smokin' hot," he says, because he can't see through my makeup. He never could. "Kym's gonna hate you."

"*Is* Kym gonna hate me?" I ask, because I'm not really sure. I've never thought so before, that she or anyone else might hate me when the makeup does its job. "For real?"

"Nah," he says, then, "well, not any more than she hates anybody else. Or a *lot* more, anyway. Definitely not any more than she hates herself. How's that?"

I want to ask why he thinks Kym Hartmann hates herself, but we probably don't have the time. So I go get my shoes, and it takes me a little while fiddling with the straps to get them to stay up at the back.

"You're sure you don't want to wear that little black dress?" Brent asks when I'm trying to find my nicer coat in the hall closet. "Everybody's gonna be dressed like that."

"Absolutely sure," I tell him. "And Kym won't be."

He tries to distract me with work drama as we take the new bypass around the north side of town. His truck still smells like the leather cleaner he used before he came to visit me in Columbus, and it's strong enough that I can't smell anything over it.

"So that's Leah," he says. He's talking about Kym's intern again, the one who has a crush on him. "And it's like it won't stop. Like she's not gonna let it go."

When we pull into the parking lot of the country club, he drives through a couple rows of cars before finding a spot over by the old pool. Dad had the first spot before the little circle dropoff, so I guess I never noticed how crowded it can get here. I don't think they put a sign there or anything, but everyone knew it was reserved for him, like a sheriff might have regular business at a country club.

"How old is she?" I ask as we're getting out.

Brent slides his arm through mine, and I tug my peacoat tighter around my chest. The wind's picked up, and there are a few leaves tumbling across the sidewalk and down the hill towards the pool.

"Who?"

"Leah. It's a college internship, isn't it? So she has to be young."

"Oh," he says. "Yeah, I guess. But I think she went back to school. Maybe after some classes at the extension or something. Not everybody knows what they wanna do right away, you know."

"Sure," I say.

Brent catches the heavy oak door and holds it open for me. Inside, the smell of old flowers—that's what I always thought it was, anyway—washes over us, and I can tell right away the country club hasn't changed since I've been here last. The carpet's the same muted florals, and the bar's still lined with cracked green leather.

Brent leaves a hand at my back as we walk down the ramp with the little gold knobs on the railing. He leans close and whispers something that's supposed to be funny, because I'm sure I look stiff now, as we funnel into the dining room.

# 22



Paige's humane society gala almost reminds me of a prom—not mine, but somewhere fancy, maybe in the 60's, full of satin shawls and big floral centerpieces with tall white feathers sticking out. There's that tension everywhere, too, tiny interactions that are all a little too meaningful and a social hierarchy you can see right away.

This is why Cody said I couldn't miss it, the chance to see all the town's major players in the same room. They move through it in that practiced way that tells you nothing's changed here in the last fifty years. The gala probably grew into what it is now the way everything else does in Paige, isolated like a diabetic's foot that's been cut off from circulation from the outside for too long. It's a show of money and power like the charity events in the city are, only more claustrophobic, and it feels a couple decades behind.

I take inventory of the families I'm supposed to know as Cody greets his old football coach. The Rolenfelds are front and center with a little extra space on either side of their table so everyone can see them. There's a network that reaches out from there then, row by row.

We're a row behind and to the right of Kara Peterson. She's at the far left of the first row, probably where Stan used to sit to MC. The tables between her and the Rolenfelds are full of the families who have houses in Rolling Fields and call into the tip hotline anytime a dirty car drives through the neighborhood or someone lets their grass get too high.

I don't recognize the other people at Kara's table, but that's probably just because I haven't stopped any of them for stumbling around the square drunk or swerving onto any freshly-mown lawns or anything. That's the baseline here. Towns like Paige have patterns, crimes you get used to. Even the city had some of this, waves and seasons for things. It's rare you get a case anywhere that really stands out, that doesn't make sense in its context.

But that's not why I'm here. There shouldn't be anything important to see at a humane society gala in Paige, Ohio.

Later, once all the prime rib and the little flower-stamped mashed potatoes have been cleared away, the waiters deliver slices of chocolate cake, and the tables start to mix a little.

Cody whispers the names of people as they come by, but most of them only glance at me before clapping him on the back or visiting with his parents or one of the other couples at our table— the high school principal and the football coach and their wives.

I watch his parents as they interact. Cody's dad's quiet, nodding every now and then the way Cody does, and his eyebrows bunch up the same way. I can see Cody got his smile from his mom, a kind one. They live a little ways outside of town, past the junction and into Dale, but they belong here at the front of the room; Stubsen told me they built most of the houses in Rolling Fields, the ones Cody's been renovating in what he calls the great Paige race for the HGTV kitchens.

The principal's wife spends some time trying to make eye contact with Maureen Rolenfeld before she finally comes over. She's making rounds now, stopping briefly at each table and weaving her way down the room like this is her party.

I'm surprised when she touches my shoulder the same way she does Cody's. It's weird to hear her voice, too, after all this time I've just seen her in the background. When she asks how I'm settling in, I say something about the community, the way you do, making it sound like the good kind.

She smiles and nods in response. Her smiles don't reach her eyes, but that's how these wives always are—beautiful but tired. It takes a lot of energy to keep track of what you're sincere about.

I look back at Kara's table once Maureen's moved on. Kara's here with Brent Thomas, just like Cody told me she would be. I keep looking in their direction whenever I get the chance, but I don't know what I'm really waiting to see until the president of the humane society board gets up to the podium and announces the big Rolenfeld donation.

There's a beat before Kara joins in the applause, and Brent reaches a hand towards her under the tablecloth. She's wearing a face like everyone tonight, foundation just a shade too dark for her skin.

I'm about to look away before anyone can notice I'm staring, but then Dalton claps Brent on the back on his way up to the mic. It's quick, casual; you wouldn't even see it if you weren't looking. He doesn't touch anyone else.

I lean closer to Cody. "Dalton and Brent Thomas. Friends?" I ask while the clapping's still too loud for anyone around us to hear.

Cody shakes his head. But he's looking at Kara's table, too, with his eyebrows bunched up.

# 23

*Kara*

By the time dinner's finished, I feel too heavy to move. It's like I'm rooted to the carpet through this chair with the knots at the back that have always dug into my shoulders. I push my cake away.

"We should dance," Brent says, his chair facing mine now.

I look around the room. The rest of our table's gone. This is the up-and-about portion of the night, the one my dad was so good at. 80's and 90's love songs are playing through some old box speakers over the dance floor, and there's a pretty good crowd there now. Dalton and Parker kicked off the dancing a little while ago, spinning for one of the guys from the paper who was kneeling down in the corner and taking pictures for the Sunday special.

Brent squeezes my knee under the table as Carla Phillips, the secretary of the humane society board, comes over. Carla was in my dad's class and always has a bunch of stories about him, but they're never stories he's told me, never stories I can imagine him in.

She bends to hug me, and I stare into her shawl and nod along for a while as she talks. I tell her at one point that I think I remember a story of me and Dad at an ice cream drive, but I'm not sure I do. Sometimes I think my memories from Paige are corrupted like files on a bad hard drive, that they've all been a little warped.

Carla's still talking when I get a whiff of peaches again, of the lotion I haven't worn since that night. My face heats up, and I try to pretend that it's from laughing, that whatever she's saying is funny, like it should be. Maybe the peaches are in her perfume. Or maybe they're everywhere in this town. Maybe Paige just reeks of that night for me now.

I focus again, trying to react normally as she segues into the usual line about how proud Dad would be of me and mistakes me for a lawyer like everyone here does.

She gives my shoulder a squeeze when she's about to move on, and I hold my breath, trying not to think about peaches as she leans close.

"Anyhoo," she says, "I'm sure glad to see you here with somebody special." She winks at me before turning to some St. Luke's ladies at the table behind us.

"Somebody special," Brent says, giving me a bigger wink and a grin once she's gone. "So, how are you holding up?"

"Fine," I tell him, but when I look around the room, my eyes land on Dalton again. I can always find him, even in a crowd.

Brent follows my eyes, turning around in his chair, then looks back at me. "You sure?" he asks.

I nod. "What'd he say to you?"

"Say?"

"On his way to the podium." I was right here, but it was like all I could hear once Dalton came towards us was the heating system and the chairs scraping against the carpet as people stood up and all the clapping. I wasn't really here for any of the silent auction winners, either, or for the donation tallies, just like I wasn't *there* when I took shots at a pool table and walked home from the Rolenfelds ten years ago or when I turned on all the lights Monday night. I hate how much effort it takes to stay here now, to not lose myself again.

Brent's shaking his head. "Nothing," he says.

"Nothing?"

He has that face on like he's worried about me, like he knows there's more to worry about. "He didn't say anything. We really should dance, you know. Look normal."

I agree, because of course that's the look I'm going for, normal. So we get up with the next song, a ballad that was before our time, and as we dance, I try to think about all the times Brent and I have done this before and to pretend tonight isn't any different. I focus on my hand on his shoulder and avoid looking over it, where I know Dalton is.

"Why do you think he did it, though?" I ask once we've drifted a little distance away from the other couples.

"What?" Brent's voice is loud in my ear.

"Slapped you on his way up to the mic."

Brent leans back and looks at me, and I think for a second that maybe I imagined this, too.

"I don't know," he says then. "Probably he's just wanting to mess with you, don't you think?"

"Maybe."

"Don't let him get to you."

I nod, and Brent runs his hand between my shoulder blades as I count all the chairs and the sounds and the smells in this place that aren't peaches.

# 24

Kara's just coming out of the ladies' room that smells like the gardenia sachets they keep in the towel dispenser when Dalton Rolenfeld rounds the corner.

He's too close for her to pass by. He's smiling, of course, even bigger than he does for the cameras.

He starts to say he's glad she's back. She spins around, but there's just the wall behind her and a little table with a silk floral arrangement on it. Nowhere for her to go.

She looks sick, Dalton says, and he asks her what's wrong. A couple seconds later, he catches her.

# 25



*Sam*

I get away from one of the humane society board ladies just a minute after I lose track of Kara. I was trying to follow her when she got up.

I scan the room, but she's not with any of the groups scattered around talking. She's not dancing, either, and Brent's sitting alone at her table.

I walk towards the little hallway at the back of the place, and of course that's where I find her slumped against the wall. I can tell it's her even with Dalton's back covering my view of her face, his arms around her.

He flinches when I yell.

"She fainted," he tells me, and I don't even look at him before I grab her.

He trips back like he was just caught in this somehow, like he walked out of the men's room and then there she was, unconscious against him.

There's a gasp somewhere behind us, loud voices, some

rustling around.

I let Kara slump down the carpet and reach for her pulse. She's conscious, or at least her eyes are open. I can see her chest rise and fall.

I've barely gotten a pulse on her wrist and haven't had a chance to ask her anything when Cody gets to us. He's already carrying her around the corner before I can stand up. I don't look at Dalton as I pass by him.

The innards of the country club are like a maze or something out of a horror film, dimly-lit hallways that all seem to lead back into each other. I snake around by the kitchens for a minute before I see a door behind a partition of fake plants that's just swinging closed.

By the time I catch up to them, Cody's picking his way along a stone path I can barely see that winds through the landscaping by the eighteenth green. He doesn't set Kara down until he gets to the parking lot.

I reach for her wrist when he steps back after laying her on a bench under the overhang. "Kara?" I ask.

She looks up, then starts to pull her hand away.

"Can you hear me, Kara?"

She nods, opening her mouth this time.

I look back at Cody. He has his phone out. "Ambulance?" he asks.

"No," she says.

I almost ignore this, but she says it again, and then again.

"I'm okay," she manages after a minute.

I look around. There's a sconce close to the door, but its light doesn't reach this far. I sit back on my heels. The concrete's torn my hose at one knee. "Can you tell me what happened?" I ask.

Kara looks at Cody, then back at the building, and I wonder if she knows how she got outside.

That's when Brent Thomas gets to us, when he pushes past me and leans over her. He's saying things, but quietly, words I can't make out. Kara's looking away now, not at any of us.

"It's okay," Brent says after a minute. Maybe it's not that long. But this isn't like the emergencies I'm used to; it feels like everything's moving too slowly.

Cody steps forward, ready to pick her up again. "Let's get her to the hospital," he says.

"It's okay," Brent repeats. "She just got a little overheated. Her dress is probably too tight."

"She's done it before?" Cody asks before I can remember what you're supposed to ask next. It's this, of course, some history that matters. Because her dress isn't tight at all.

Brent shakes his head. "She just needs some air," he says.

So we give her air, for now. Cody leaves, jogging across the parking lot to pull around his truck.

I look at the front door again. People will be out soon to see what's going on. This was the highlight of the gala, I'm sure, the thing they'll all be talking about tomorrow at The Strawberry even if none of them know what really happened. I can hear some voices down by the side door already. They'll see us if we can't move her soon.

I kneel down beside the bench again and try to ask Kara all the questions I'm supposed to now, about what she remembers.

Her voice is low, but she's coherent. She remembers going to the bathroom. She remembers going to the hallway. She's still lying back, Brent's arm around her shoulders, and she's holding onto his other hand like she might fall off the bench without it.

"She's okay," Brent repeats, but he keeps an arm behind her when she finally sits up on her own, looking like she could collapse again anytime.

About twenty minutes later, Kara's propped up in an old leather recliner in her living room, and Brent's in the kitchen. He knows the place, obviously, wrapped her in a blanket and got her water and turned on all the lights.

She said as soon as we got her inside that she just got dizzy, but there are tear tracks down her makeup I can see in this light, and the skin across her chest and the backs of her arms are blotchy. She hasn't said anything yet about Dalton Rolenfeld.

I look around the living room and try to get a sense of how she's been living. There's a stack of coats by the closet, but the coffee table's clear, and a quilt's folded neatly over the back of the sofa. There are only a few movies in the media cabinet, and I make out some sitcoms and a Disney boxed set—no thrillers or anything that looks too dark.

I kneel down on the pretense of pulling off her heels and ask her again if I can take her to the hospital, or at least file a report. I keep asking, thinking she might change her mind.

"It looked like an assault," I tell her. "I saw Dalton holding onto you. They'd believe me."

She shakes her head, says, "I'm okay."

I wait, because of course she's not okay.

"I could call ahead," I say after we've been quiet for a minute. "I'd tell them it's from low blood pressure or something, so there wouldn't be any talk." Though I'm not sure what they'd be looking for at the ER, exactly; her dress isn't torn or anything. But she's in shock, and you don't just slide into shock when you step out of a bathroom.

Brent comes around the chair, and I have to back away. He has a mug of coffee for her this time. "I'll stay with her tonight," he says. "I'll call if anything happens."

Kara looks up and catches my eyes. She's at least more alert now.

"Thank you," she tells me again. "And please thank Cody."

Cody's waiting for me outside, standing by his truck with his cell phone in his hand.

"She's okay?" he asks as soon as the door closes behind me.

"She's coherent," I tell him, because 'okay' is still a ways off.

"Brent said she'd had panic attacks. Before, I mean. You really think that was what it was?"

I shake my head, and he opens the passenger door to his truck before I can reach for it.

"It looked like an assault," I say as soon as he's around the hood and inside. "Dalton Rolenfeld was holding her up against the wall when I found her."

Cody lets out a long breath and doesn't take his eyes off the road the whole drive to my place.

When we get there, I check the handle before I unlock my front door and turn on the lights as soon as I get inside. It takes me a while going through some boxes in the linen closet to find the bottle of Xanax I still haven't needed to refill. I cut one in half and take it with a glass of water before I go to bed, thinking Kara and I will probably both have nightmares tonight.

# 26



*Sebastian's mom*

I want to say I didn't see what happened, but I was only a feet away when Cody carried Kara out of the country club. Her head was lolling off his arm, her face white as a sheet.

I can't stop thinking about her face as I get ready for bed. When I'm out of the shower, I check the driveway for my son again. He's still not home. But that's how he is; I don't get to ask where he goes or why anymore. There are things he hides, just like his father. Or maybe he gets that from me.

Later on, when I can't sleep, I come out to the kitchen for a cup of tea and find myself looking at the staircase. I've been thinking about it a lot when he's gone. His room's just at the top. I don't know what I'm afraid I'd find there.

I tell myself this feeling's from reading too many mysteries, or maybe it's from living with his father for so long. Maybe this is normal, even, with an adult child. After a while, you don't really know them anymore. And I used to think I knew his dad so well.

I've almost talked myself into going up the stairs—just to stop thinking about it, to prove to myself how silly I'm being—when I imagine I hear a car coming up the drive. I look out the window, but there aren't any lights.

I don't work up the guts to do it tonight. I lie in bed for a couple hours before I take a sedative and hope to dream of anything but Kara Peterson's face.

# 27

*Kara*

Sunday morning, Bev comes over before she leaves for church. She and Brent are taking turns watching me after last night, like there's some new risk inherent to just being in my own body right now and I can't be trusted to know when it's going to get me.

Bev at least has a good pretense this time, delivering a taco dish and a pie she baked—her blackberry cobbler, one of my favorites.

"This is just Gleson's crust," she warns me as I slide the containers into the refrigerator, "nothing special."

I thank her and rearrange some milk and sandwiches Gleson's packs in the deli. I stock up on food now like I'm going to be here for a while, like they say people do down in Cincinnati when they think it's going to snow, with eggs and milk and bread and a bunch of more perishable, prepared things like I might forget how to feed myself, too.

Bev walks past me to fold the blanket we left on the sofa. Brent and I spent the night there with the floodlights on outside and old Disney DVD's playing on the TV like we used to when we were teenagers.

"You're feeling okay?" Bev asks.

"Fine," I tell her.

"You're sure?"

"You saw."

"It wasn't that bad," she says. "The story's how that hallway's always hot and you'd just been dancing and got overheated. You probably did them a favor, you know. They need a new central air system. That side of the building's always like a furnace with the heat on. Maybe they'll finally redo those ducts like they've been talking about for forever."

"Yeah," I say, like that's what this could be about, duct work. "It was probably the heat."

Bev picks up a glass in the sink and fills it with soapy water. "You're not..." She stops. "You're not eating normally."

I try to laugh as I wet a paper towel. I've spent the time since Brent left wiping dust out of a few empty drawers. "You're not asking if I'm pregnant, are you?"

Bev shakes her head, but she's not smiling. "No. No, of course not. I was just...I heard Dalton was there. When you passed out, I mean."

I take the paper towel to the cabinet that used to hold all of Mom's magazines. Hers were all beautiful tiled pools and too-tidy family rooms and sweeping rose gardens. Not like Dad's.

Bev follows me across the kitchen. "I know it's stressful for you being back like this," she says, "and with him on TV and everything, and right across..." She looks behind us at the windows, then back at the sink with all the dishes. Brent and I made a big pile of them last night, ice cream and cereal bowls and a bunch of glasses of water like I might dehydrate otherwise, like that was the risk.

I want to say I haven't been thinking about Dalton at all, like I used to say I wasn't thinking about my mom after she died, but Bev could always see through me.

"I've been worried about you," she says.

As I wipe out the magazine cabinet, I try to convince her I'm okay. Or that I should be.

"You're...you're sure it was Dalton, aren't you?" she asks me after a minute.

I stop moving the paper towel, barely covered with a layer of dust now, as I think about how to answer this. "Yeah," I tell her then, looking up. "I am."

"I'm sorry," Bev says. She takes up a piece of cobbler after a few minutes and insists I eat it, saying something about my blood sugar.

We stand together at the island for a while trying to make small talk about anything but Dalton and last night, the dirty paper towel crumpled into a ball beside me. She asks about things with the house and what I'm wearing to the dinner for Dad and if I need any help with the arrangements.

"That's the train," she says when the whistle blows out by the junction. "I guess I should get going. You're not up for church today, are you?"

I tell her I'm not, like usual.

She nods and picks up her purse. "I'll say you're feeling better, that I checked you out myself and you just got too warm. That'll stop any gossip."

After Bev leaves, I wait for the whistle out by town, the one that always comes a few minutes later.

Then I have to sit down. Maybe it's my blood sugar, like she said. The trains haven't changed. You get used to them, if you live here long enough, and don't even wake up when they come through at night. Like the one that comes just after three in the morning or the one that comes at 11:11 on the dot. I used to sit up waiting for it when I was a kid.

It was 11:10 when I saw the numbers on the bedside clock, and I heard everything that happened afterwards. There wasn't a train whistle that night.

I go for my phone. I charged it in the powder room last night while we were watching *Cinderella*.

I've just gotten it unplugged when I see the peach lotion sitting out by the hand soap.

# 28



*Sam*

I meet Kara at The Strawberry again Monday over my lunch break. I called yesterday afternoon to ask her here—just to catch up, I told her, like we needed to gossip about who wore what dress Saturday night and not who went unconscious trapped in a hallway with her rapist—but she has something new for me, too.

I've seen these patterns before, of course, and know how memory works after trauma. The little balloons in Kara's brain full of that night won't stop leaking once they start. No one thought about this when it happened, though, tried to check in with her a few days afterwards or asked her about the timeline, questioned whether she remembered everything or if there were some blank spots. There's no telling how much more she'll remember now that she's home, how much more there *is* to remember.

"So you would have heard the train," I say once the waitress has dropped off my tea and Kara's coffee.

She nods. "Every night, always at the same time." She sounds sure of this, too, like she's been sure about everything else. I'm surprised she's still sure of anything. Usually, someone like Dalton Rolenfeld takes that away first.

"So that wasn't when it happened, then," I say, "a little after eleven." And of course that's all the video footage we have of him.

Kara picks up her coffee. "I remember the numbers so well, though—a bunch of them. It started at 11:10."

"The clock was changed," I say first, then, "or maybe it just wasn't right. Maybe the power went out sometime and no one changed it since it was in a guest room. Or maybe they never put it on daylight savings." But it was probably changed. This was planned. The defense would try to spin doubt about Kara's memory in a trial, but there are only so many ways this story can go. It was Dalton who grabbed her, Dalton who held her down. It doesn't really matter when he did it.

"You'd already thought of that," Kara says, not really asking.

"Sure. It was the only way he could have been outside then."

Kara looks surprised, like maybe she didn't think I believed her about Dalton. This is a pattern, too; when they're not believed by other people, victims start not to believe themselves, not to trust their own memories.

The waitress comes back to set the table next to ours, and we make small talk until she disappears behind the partition again. I want to avoid asking Kara about the gala, to keep this lunch inane, friendly. But it's all I've been able to think about since Saturday night, what I missed in that hallway, what I might have seen if I'd gotten there just a few seconds earlier.

I get my chance when she brings it up, thanking me and Cody

again for taking her home.

"Would you have reported it, if he *had* assaulted you?" I ask.

"I would." She's thought about it.

"Did he say anything to you?"

"It was all my idea."

I look up when the bell on the door chimes and one of the Rolling Fields women comes in with her husband. "What was?" I ask.

"That's what he said. That it was all his idea." She says it calmly, like she's reading it from the specials board over the hostess station. Maybe these words don't hit her like they do me, don't have the same meaning to her. Or maybe she's known this all along, about Dalton.

I take a sip of my tea, harder to swallow this time as the honey—too much honey, again—coats my throat. "You still think someone else was involved, though," I say.

"I always thought someone else was there."

"Sebastian."

"I know it's nothing to go on."

I keep an eye on the door, watching for people coming this way as we talk through the possibilities she's already considered a thousand times. I'm glad we're doing it here, at least. This is a conversation I can't have at the office, one I don't want Stubsen to overhear. There are always secrets you keep, some little conflict in what you believe versus what you're supposed to do or in what you're so sure of versus what you can prove. But there aren't any new possibilities today. Kara doesn't have any answers.

She thanks me at the end and apologizes again for all the trouble Saturday like she could have done something to stop this.

I'm alone when I get back to the office. I should be annoyed all the guys seem to do more drive-throughs at the milkshake place than paperwork, but I'm not sorry to have the station to myself now.

I open the folder with Kara's file on my computer, ready to read it again just in case this new information about the time fits in somewhere with her statement at the hospital or with the interviews with witnesses. Then I'll add notes in the notepad I keep in my purse.

Before I read, though, I check the log in the upper corner, the one that tells me who's opened the file last.

I think it's going to be Stubsen, but it's not. Before me, the case was last accessed on March fourth of this year, by Stan Peterson.

I remember the date because it was day of my first interview, the one with him when I didn't get a callback. And then he died four days later.

I *x* out of the file and sit back in my chair. Then I shut down my computer for the day and go for Kara Peterson's rape kit.

# 29



*Kara*


As soon as Brent goes into work Monday morning, I open my laptop at the kitchen table and google 'disassociation.' It's been a while since I've done this, but I want to think it's a good sign that there's a word for it, that they're just *episodes* I'm having and not someone I'm turning into.

I keep reading on and off through Tuesday afternoon, and by then, I have a text document open with a list of the things I can't remember—the shots at Dalton's party and getting home, and then turning on the lights that first week back and putting the peach lotion in the powder room sometime around the gala.

I feel like I should be able to trace at least the lotion. Brent, Sam, and Cody were all here at some point that night; one of them might have seen me move it. But of course asking makes me sound even crazier than I feel. I don't remember finding it or putting it on, but I've smelled it at least a couple times since I've been home.

I check the fridge for more clues—things I might have eaten that I don't remember or things I might have bought. I didn't count how many yogurts I picked up on my last grocery trip, though, or how many pieces of toast I've had or bowls of cereal. I'll start counting this time, keep the text document open on my laptop so I don't miss anything. I want to think I can control it like this, that these episodes can't happen when you're watching for them.

Before I head to Gleson's, I order one of those watches from Amazon that count your steps, and then I do my face like I used to here, with extra blush and eyeshadow.

I change my mind and wash it all off before I go, scrubbing my skin raw with an old washcloth and trying not to think about what I might still be missing.

I don't remember it's election day until I'm almost to town. I take a side road to avoid Clay Street, where there's already a line of cars waiting to pull into the high school to vote, and I get to Gleson's just before it starts to get busy when the factory lets out.

I focus on what I can count, then—eight individual yogurts, two each of single serve lasagnas and canned soups and milks. There are funny little frozen chocolate muffin tops I haven't seen before that say they're full of vitamins, so I get two of those, too, and three each of apples, pears, and green bean steamers.

I'm almost to the checkout lane when Becky Lange materializes in the wine aisle.

She says my name too loudly for me to pretend I don't hear. So I stop, and we hug and put on the same show I put on with her daughter here last week.

I recognize her perfume—different from Parker's, more floral—from her sitting a pew in front of ours at St. Mark's for the first fourteen years of my life. Her half-hugs are the same, too; she's one of those Paige women who won't ever change.

"I've been hopin' to run into you," she says. "How are things goin' with the house?"

"Good," I tell her, and then add a "slow" so she doesn't think she's going to get it anytime soon. She's my only choice, of course, the only real estate office in Paige, but I want to be on my way back to the city when I finally turn it over. It feels personal, letting someone like Becky Lange into your house, even if it's not really yours anymore.

"Good, good," she says, waving at someone over my shoulder.

I'm about to say something to wrap this up and move past her when she stops me. "You know we really need to get together to talk about the dinner," she says.

I focus on the half wall of magazines and the rainbow of chewing gums in the lane ahead of me. "I think we're all ready," I say. "Thank you."

Her smile doesn't budge. "What were you gonna do for chairs?"

"Chairs? Are there not still..."

"It's okay," she says, waving a hand and wafting more perfume my way. "I'll take care of it. We'll get those ones from the sanctuary we use for Christmas, nice and comfy. You don't want those ugly folded ones."

I start to say that the regular chairs in the multipurpose room are fine, that I wanted to keep this casual. But I know it really doesn't matter what I say now.

"So you're doin' okay?" she asks.

"Good, thanks." I almost tell her about running into Parker the last time I was here and lie and say this was nice, too.

She looks to the side, frowning at a younger couple I don't recognize in the cereal aisle. "Well, don't worry about the chairs," she says. "I know you've got a lot on your plate. You've had a lot of drama 'round you."

I shake my head like maybe I could argue with this.

She pats my arm before she goes, and says, "It just follows some people, I guess."

I don't know why it hits me at the cash register, why I'm just now feeling like everyone in Gleson's is looking at me. I suddenly want to cry or scream or just run to my dad's truck and keep driving until I get back to the city, where I remember everything I do and there's never any drama that has anything to do with me. It's Becky Lange and the way the cash register girl looks at me and that my dad still has a grocery tab here.

I make it through the checkout, at least, but tears are burning the corners of my eyes when I bump my cart into the automatic doors as I hurry outside.

I'm not looking ahead, or maybe I just can't see well, when I run into Cody Muller.

As we stop and I sputter out an apology, I wonder if we've been introduced properly before. But we pretend we know each other now, the way you do.

"I'm glad I ran into you," he says.

"I'm sorry," I tell him again. "I ran into *you*."

He reaches for my cart. "You feelin' okay?" he asks. "Sam said she had a good lunch with you yesterday."

"Fine," I say, and wonder what constitutes a good lunch when you're talking about a rape.

Cody takes the bags from my cart, then pushes it into all the others in the return lane. "Let me walk you out," he says.

I get the eggs on top of the bag closest to me and balance the carton between my hands as I fall into step beside him. He knows which my dad's truck is, of course, like everyone here seems to.

I guess whatever was getting me inside is stalled now, distracted. The tears won't come until later, I think. But maybe I don't know myself that well anymore.

I try to apologize for Saturday and thank Cody again, but he waves me off.

"How's the house comin' along?" he asks.

"Slow. But fine, you know, good." Like I'm supposed to be.

"Let me know if I can give you a hand with anything," he says.

I thank him. He has the passenger door of the truck open then, and I watch as he lays the bags on the floor.

He steps back once he's closed the door. "Really," he says. "I'm right around the corner now workin' on the Leeson's sunroom."

I think about Martha's add-on Brent mentioned when we were driving home and picture the multi-colored glow of her Christmas lights that used to dance across my bedroom window. It's funny how these things hit me, happy memories here, too. Martha always had those big, old-fashioned lights, giant bulbs you can't get anymore. I should have gotten in touch with her as soon as I came home.

"How's Martha?" I ask.

"Great. Up in Akron with her daughter now. I don't know if you heard, but she's expecting. Bree. So I'm hopin' to have the sunroom done when she comes home in December."

"That's great," I say. "That home was always so pretty." I can imagine a big sunroom overlooking Martha's rose garden and her grandkids darting around her potted plants at Christmas. I wonder if this is what my life would have looked like, too, if things had gone differently. Maybe I would have built on a sunroom of my own and grown into a family like I always used to think I would in these woods.

"Yeah." Cody nods. "Do you feel safe?" he asks when I'm about to thank him again.

"Safe?" It comes out like I don't know what it means.

He looks out at the traffic backing up on Fourth Street. "By yourself, I mean, out there in the woods."

"I...yes. I think so."

"Good," he says. "If you ever need anything, call, okay?"

We exchange numbers, and he's standing outside the automatic doors to Gleson's when I pull out of the parking lot.

# 30

*Sam*

About an hour before the guys should get back from patrol Tuesday night, I'm sorting through the coroner's records in the room down the hall. It's probably a waste of my time, but I don't have anything better to do now, and I'll tell the others I'm just doing research—health outcomes research, maybe, that they won't ask me about—if any of them get back early and find me here.

Copies of death certificates and autopsy notes are all shoved into the manila folders without any timeline, so all the *P*'s are together for a bunch of years. The room's not firesafe; this could all be lost so easily.

When I find Stan Peterson's folder, it's already 4:30. His copies are just a handful of sheets stapled together, the death certificate on top and some pages with numbers from the autopsy. It was a heart attack like Stubsen said, but he was only 61 and just had a couple of removed moles and borderline blood sugar noted otherwise.

The rest of the numbers don't mean anything to me. So I take the papers out to the copy machine in the main room, keeping an eye on the double doors. The automatic lights in the hallway haven't kicked on in a while. They should let me know if someone's coming, I think, with how dark it is outside already.

I watch the light flash from under the scanner and fold the copies to fit them into an envelope. I did the same with the files in Kara's rape kit yesterday and sent them with the DNA sample to Lisa, my friend at the lab in Cincinnati.

I return the original autopsy report and am back at my desk when Stubsen gets in from patrol at ten till five.


"You watchin' the election, Ellis?" Stubsen asks as soon as the guys have broken up in the kitchen later that evening.

I look at the TV screen like this is what I've been doing all afternoon and focus on the numbers rolling across the bottom. Rolenfeld's pulling over sixty percent now, just an hour before the polls close. The final count won't be in for at least a few hours, but it's looking positive for Paige. Or at least Paige will act like it; Dalton's probably not a good choice for most of the people who live around here.

Stubsen takes his usual seat on the corner of my desk. "The party's Friday, you know," he says.

I look back at my computer and pretend to be focused on some random paperwork I pulled up. "Are you still running security for them?"

"Yeah, absolutely."

"That must be a big headache," I say, "with all the political stuff."

"What do you mean?"

I lean back in my chair and look around the room before meeting his eyes. "It's at the house, isn't it? The party?"

"Yeah, a big one. Lots a press there."

When I look back at the TV, the camera's live on Dalton somewhere in Columbus. That's something about him winning, I guess; there will be more cameras on him. I always think that's what we need, to have a camera on every rapist 24/7.

Stubsen shifts on my desk. "You don't think somebody'd do somethin' to…"

I don't wait for him to guess. "Spy on him," I finish.

Stubsen opens his mouth again.

"I'd be worried about privacy," I say. "You know, that someone could plant a camera somewhere or something. You were saying the other day there were cameras that didn't even have to connect to the internet, weren't you? That could go anywhere, and you couldn't trace where they were sending the feed?"

Stubsen's jaw goes slack. "Yeah. That's right, usin' a VPN. That's what I was tellin' you, about how they can hide where you're on the computer."

"VPN," I echo. "But I guess that must be hard to get, and the camera'd have to connect to something to get set up, wouldn't it?"

Stubsen shakes his head, and his chin wobbles a bit. His neck's like a tree trunk; that little flap under his jaw's the only part that ever moves. "Not hard at all," he says. Then he comes to my side of the desk, reaching around me to type on my keyboard. I hold my breath until he steps back again.

A bunch of VPN providers load up on my screen, promising

security, privacy, untraceability.

"Wow," I say. "I had no idea something like that was so accessible. And the cameras? Could anyone do that, too?"

Stubsen nods and leans forward again.

I watch the next search results load and let him talk about satellites for a while.

# 31

*Sebastian*

The crowd's too loud to really hear his speech at the capital, but I know what he's saying anyway, about hard work and loyalty and America. Sure, the words don't mean anything, but Dalton's a winner; he doesn't need any of that shit. And what *could* he say, even if he were telling the truth? That he won because he's rich, and rich people can take whatever they want?

I have another beer as I watch. There's no talk of any of the rumors, anything I thought might have come up by now. But I knew he was bulletproof, that he'd get through whatever they threw at him. Even Kara.

I'm alone tonight, and I lock my door before getting the tissues and the sound machine. I like to hear crickets now, like that night. And this is a celebration.

I'm only a little pissed that Dalton took so much credit at the gala; at least the crickets were *my* idea, not his.

# 32

*Sam*

When I get to the office Wednesday morning, there's already a crowd around the coffee pot. The guys are adding that powder to their mugs like always, bulking up and waking up or whatever they think Stubsen's doing. They still look away when I catch their eyes. This will always be a good ol' boys club, the same as when Sheriff Stan was running it; I know I'm only here because of pressure on Baer, since he didn't have the same privileges Peterson had accrued through his career. But this is how it always is, in any field. You can't change the culture as quickly as you can institute a quota.

"Ellis." Stubsen breaks rank as soon as he sees me and almost beats me to my desk. "You heard about Rolenefeld? I know you don't watch much TV, but..."

"I get the news," I tell him. And some kind of congratulatory message was on every automated billboard in town this morning. It would have been hard to miss.

"'s pretty sweet, huh? Second generation from right here and all that."

"Sweet," I echo.

"Anyway, like I said, I'm doin' security at the party Friday night. Should be huge. You'll come by?"

"Maybe," I tell him. "But I have a lot going on. I'm redecorating my place."

"Yeah? Whatcha doin?"

I make up some things that wouldn't interest him, about replacing bathroom tile and pulling up carpets and repainting. I've actually thought about doing these things, though, like I might stick around.

Stubsen grins, pointing a finger at me. "*That's* why Cody Muller's always with you. He's doin' that stuff at your place?"

"Right," I say. Or at least I've let him fix a screen door and a couple cabinets. So far.

Stubsen nods, then focuses on my desk for a couple seconds. "You don't think Kara's gonna make any trouble, do you? For the party or anything?"

"Kara? No."

He glances over his shoulder at the others still talking in the kitchen, then lowers his voice. "I told Dalton about what you said. He's gonna get Wagner and Schmitt, too, to keep a watch out on everybody at the house."

"Good," I say. "You can't be too careful with a crowd that size."

Stubsen's about to say something else when my phone buzzes in my purse. It's Lisa.

I slide the toggle and put her on hold, something Lisa and I have both done a lot over the years in offices like this one.

Stubsen leans closer, looking for Cody's name.

"It's Lisa, my friend," I tell him, and try to smile. "Girl chat."

Stubsen nods, and I take the call off hold as I walk out into the hallway.

"Sorry," I tell her.

"A guy at work?" Lisa asks.

"What else?"

She laughs, and I can picture her eye roll. These things have always rolled off of Lisa better than they have me.

"So you have the rape kit?" I ask.

"I ran it," she says. "I'm sorry, though, there isn't a match in the system."

"Thanks. I didn't think so."

There's a pause. "You're thinking of someone, though."

I take a few more steps down the hallway, where I can see into the office through the little window with that diamond mesh that's supposed to prevent it from shattering. Stubsen's back at the coffee pot, waving his arms around as the other guys laugh at whatever he's saying.

"I don't know."

"Come on," Lisa says. "Is it that politician? Rolenfeld?"

"He was holding her down, but I think there was someone else there." It should be obvious who it was. It was premeditated, planned well. I'm just missing it.

"You have an idea who?" Lisa asks.

I watch Stubsen for a few more seconds and wonder where his line with women is, the difference between not knowing how to interact with them and hating them for it, wanting to get back at them.

"Does your district collect staff DNA? To keep in the system, I mean?"

"From officers? Shit," she says. "You really are thinking of somebody."

"A little," I admit. "But it's a shot in the dark."

"We don't. It's some kind of rights thing, I think."

"Probably they don't here, then, either," I say, and Lisa and I catch up for another couple minutes before she has to go.

# 33



*Kara*

I can see some light through the trees, but I don't hear music from the Rolenfeld place. Tonight's not like high school or college, like the parties Dalton used to throw when his parents were both in Washington. This one's quieter, but I'm sure there are cars lined up along Meridian all the way back to town. They'll leave tracks of mud off the sides of the asphalt tomorrow.

I try not to look at the windows when the light shifts through the trees. I check my fitness watch again, instead, but the graph of my steps hasn't changed; I haven't been wandering off or anything, forgetting big things like I still worry I might.

Brent's at the Rolenfeld party with Bev, celebrating with champagne and finger foods from Hart's catering. To keep up appearances, we decided, and to make it look like there's nothing wrong, nothing to draw attention to me. I'm probably the only person in town who won't stop by. Bev and Brent will tell anyone who asks that I'm having allergy trouble that gave me a migraine. That's what Bev came up with a long time ago, for all the other things I wasn't here for, and all that matters is that it sounds true.

It's the valley and the mold on the corn; there's no one here who doesn't have some kind of allergy trouble.

I try to eat one of the frozen chocolate muffin tops from Gleson's—one of three—but my stomach's sour. It's guilt now, I think, for not doing more, for not doing *something*, at least, to expose Dalton before he got to Washington. I wonder sometimes if no one else sees what he is. It seems so obvious to me, like everyone should know, but it's just his name that matters here in Paige. I guess that's all that mattered to the rest of the state, too.

I'm sitting up in my dad's bed with the TV on *Golden Girls* for some distraction, about half of the muffin top still in its plastic dish beside me, when I hear the scratching.

I tell myself I'm going to catch it this time. Then I'll know what it is, and it won't bother me again. They say your imagination's always worse.

It's a branch, I think, and I say this out loud. It has to be, the wind hitting it just right that it comes and goes.

Then I hear it again, with a soft *tap tap tap* this time. It sounds like it's coming from outside the living room, and I walk over to the bedroom door, still locked.

It's been quiet for a couple minutes when I finally open the door. Then I rush down the staircase and turn on all the outside lights, scanning the windows, but of course there's no one out there.

The scratching's stopped. I wonder for a few seconds if it was in my head, if I can control it with the lights.

But then the crickets are loud, so loud that I can't hear the TV upstairs anymore.

I run to the powder room, throwing up into the waste basket when I don't make it to the toilet in time.

The crickets are screeching now, screaming in my head.

It's not until I hear the scratching again, this time on the wall right outside the bathroom, that I think to use my phone.

# 34

Cody's pounding his fist against the door like he's going to knock it down. "Kara?" he yells. "It's Cody. Can you hear me?"

There's no noise inside. He tries to look in through the kitchen window, but the floodlight turns the glass into a mirror.

He beats on the door again. "Kara? Sam said there was..."

He stops when the door opens and he sees her face.

Kara slams into his chest, and he half-drags her back across the threshold, only stopping to lock the door behind him. He takes her to the recliner where they put her after the gala. She's moving her legs on her own this time, but her face is red and beaded with sweat.

He only leaves her for a second to walk along the row of tall windows that look out toward the Rolenfeld's land. But there's nothing out there. And of course she hasn't told him what he should be looking for, exactly.

"Let me get you some water," he says. "Or we can go straight to town, to the hospital. Whatever you..."

She's shaking her head. It takes her a minute to say something. "I'm sorry," she tells him then, sitting up. "I'm okay."

Cody's in the kitchen now, several paces away from her. "Sam'll be here soon," he says a couple times. He finds a glass in one of the cabinets, an old football tumbler, but he keeps looking over his shoulder at Kara.

They're quiet for a minute while he runs the tap.

"I imagined them." Her voice is weak, soft, but it stops his hand on the faucet.

He turns around. "What did you see?"

"Heard," she says. "Just scratching, and then crickets." Then she starts crying, big heaves that don't produce any tears.

He goes over and sets the glass down on the table next to her. He doesn't try to touch her. He just stands there, waiting.

# 35



*Kara*

Sam's in front of me now, kneeling by the recliner and asking questions. She's gone back some hours with these, to what I ate for dinner and how much water I've had to drink and what kind of work I was doing on my computer this afternoon.

I think she's trying to make sure I didn't have a stroke or something, but it feels good to remember these things, to know that everything made sense until the crickets started screaming. Maybe it would have been better, that this would be easier if it had been a stroke.

She hands me the glass of water from the table, and I take another sip, because I'm telling myself maybe it was just dehydration, this delusion I'm wanting so badly to be something else.

"And you haven't gotten anything new," she says. "No more notes."

"Notes?" Cody asks from behind me. "You got a note?"

"In Columbus," I say, twisting to look at him, but he's already opening the front door.

When he comes back in, he's holding an envelope.

Sam's up, then, across the room. She asks me if it's okay to open it—it's not sealed, she says, like the last one was—and when I agree, she stands there for a second with Cody reading over her shoulder.

I count heartbeats, breaths, planks of wood on the floor. "What is it?" I ask when I think it's been too long.

Sam looks up. "Are you sure..." She pauses before she walks it over to me.

The writing's the same as the first one, on plain white copy paper. *You'll get what's coming to you.*

Sam starts to say the things cops do then, about looking into this, about all the ways they can keep me safe and how common threats like these are and how rarely anything ever comes of them.

I nod along. I don't know how to tell her I'm not as scared as she thinks I am, though. This is relief I'm feeling now, relief that there was at least one thing that was real tonight, one thing that wasn't in my head. My head couldn't have produced an envelope. But it still doesn't sound real, does it? It seems so cheesy, so cliché, *what's coming to me.*

"Where was it?" she asks Cody. I turn to look at him, too.

He's staring out the kitchen window and doesn't turn around. "On the doorstep."

"Just now?" Sam asks. "Do you remember seeing it..."

"It was there when I came. I saw it, but I didn't think anything of it." He looks back at Sam. "I'm sure," he tells her. "I stepped over it."

A little while later, we're back on questions about tonight, about what I heard and who I didn't see coming right to my front door.

Sam's kneeling on the carpet by the recliner again, and Cody's standing to the side, just a step or two behind.

"You heard crickets," he says. "That's what you said when I came in."

I look down. My arms are blotchy in this light, probably like my face is. They look almost like hives, but flat. "They couldn't have been real," I say.

"Just crickets?" Sam asks.

"Right."

"When did it start?"

"I don't know."

"What were you doing?" Sam tries. "Do you remember what you were doing?

"I was in bed. Watching *Golden Girls*."

Sam looks at Cody. I look at my hands.

"I know they can't be that loud," I say, "crickets."

Sam shakes her head. "Noises seem louder when you're under stress, and when…"

"It's not the first time something hasn't lined up." The tears start again, quiet ones this time, but they shake my whole body. I can't stop. But I have to let them out, to tell someone before Brent gets back from the party and sees me like this.

I try to swallow. "I don't remember how I got home."

"Tonight?" Sam asks. "Were you out..."

I shake my head. "That night. I don't remember anything until I woke up the next morning."

"Your dad was out of town?"

"Right. At that training weekend they always have in December."

"Of course," she says. "And no one said anything afterwards, about helping you get back to your house or seeing you leave or anything like that?"

"I wasn't drunk." I can't look at her when I say this. Because what if I was?

"No," she says.

It's quiet for a few minutes, and I try to count things I can see, DVD's this time.

"That can happen with trauma," Sam tells me. "All kinds of trauma. It's common."

"I want to remember it."

She looks at the door, then back at Cody.

"It hasn't happened any more, the forgetting?" she asks. "Nothing more recent?"

I look out the window, at the big maple outside. There's a beat of quiet before Cody says something.

"Was the TV still on?" he asks.

"What?"

"When you heard the crickets. Could you hear them even with

the TV on?"

I nod. "And then scratching. No, the scratching was first. At a window, I thought, down here. And then at that bathroom." I point to the hallway off the kitchen.

"You heard that over the TV?" Sam asks, but Cody's already out the front door again.

# 36

When Cody finishes his walk around the outside of the house, he motions Sam over to the hallway by the powder room.

"There's nothin' out there that could scratch the house," he says as soon as they're out of earshot. "No branches or anything."

Kara's still staring straight ahead at the living room windows. There's still nothing out there.

Sam nods. "I think she must have had a panic attack. With the party, and…"

"That party's been goin' on for hours. Why now?"

"I don't know."

"While she was just watchin' TV?"

"They don't always come when you think they should," Sam says, but she doesn't sound sure.

There aren't any crickets singing when Sam and Cody finally leave Kara with Brent in the early hours of the morning. That's how crickets are, though. They stop when they sense a predator, when they feel any vibration at all. That's why you have to sneak up on them.

37

*Sam*

I come to the station Saturday morning even though I'm not on the schedule. I tell myself it's just to talk to Baer about Kara, but the truth is that I'm a little like all the guys lingering around Stubsen in the break room today, wanting to be the first to hear his take on the Rolenfeld party. It's not that I trust Stubsen, really, but that he might say something he doesn't mean to, drop some clue without knowing it.

I listen from my desk, not sure yet exactly what I'm hoping to hear. My back's to all of them, but Stubsen's voice bounces off the concrete walls as he goes on about how much champagne Dalton served and how many reporters were there and all the politicians from the capitol he'd only seen on TV before last night.

I keep listening from down the hall as I'm filing Kara's newest note with the rest of her case in the evidence locker. I've photocopied it already and uploaded it in an email to Baer. He's late getting in, at least half an hour past his usual time. This keeps getting later. He's going to Florida in a couple weeks, and it's like he's trying to ease us into his not being here so we won't notice

157

when he doesn't show up at all.

Stubsen comes over as soon as I'm back at my desk. "Whoa, Ellis," he says. "Thought you were off today."

"Not today," I tell him, because he won't check.

"I didn't see you at the party."

"I was next door. Kara Peterson got another note."

"That's not right," he says, right away. "Dalton was at the house all night. Never let him outta my sight."

"I know."

"Did you bring it with you? Is it…"

"I filed it. We'll have to send it to a specialist."

Stubsen sits down on his usual corner of my desk. "Specialist?" he asks.

"For handwriting analysis."

"I don't think we do that," he says, then, after a breath, "You really think somebody's gonna hurt her?"

I meet his eyes and wonder if Stubsen could be as dim as he seems. Maybe he's too dim to be involved, even in some small way. Or maybe this is all an act, how he gets overlooked.

"We need to increase patrol there at night," I tell him.

"I don't know Baer'll go for that."

I nod, but I don't really give a shit what Baer will go for. So I ask Stubsen about the party, instead, if there was any trouble.

"Nothin' at all," he tells me. "A lot of drinkin' from the locals, but nothin' outta the ordinary."

"No one unhappy? No mention of Kara?"

"Huh uh. I'm in on Monday," he says. "Want me to make sure

Baer gets to the note first thing?"

I twist to look at Baer's office. "He won't be in today?"

"Off for the weekend," Stubsen says.

I'm about to tell him I'll change the night patrol orders myself when my phone buzzes in my purse. It's Lisa. I hold it up to Stubsen so he can see the name.

"Hey," I say, sliding the toggle when I get out to the hallway.

"Sorry," she says. "It's been crazy here. But I looked over the autopsy you sent."

I wait, making my way down the hall to the little window.

"Is it a different case?" she asks. "Than the rape?"

"Probably not a case," I admit. "I just thought you might see something I wouldn't."

"I'd bet on caffeine."

"Caffeine?" I don't know why it stops me. I guess I didn't really think there would be anything suspicious in Stan's autopsy. I look through the glass, and my eyes land on Stubsen. He's just finished refilling his coffee.

"108 milligrams per liter in his blood," Lisa says.

"That's a lot?"

"Like a coffee or a soda by itself would bring it to about six." There's a pause. "You really didn't think this was a case? It's connected, isn't it, to the rape kit?"

"Maybe," I tell her. Then I try to change the subject as I watch Stubsen leave through the big double doors.

# 38



*Kara*

Bev's feeling under the weather Saturday night and has to cancel our dinner at The Slice, so Brent brings by some Mexican—Paco's, this time, like I'm used to—in her stead. We've fallen into this time at home together like we haven't missed anything since I lived here, like the last decade and a half hasn't been broken up by phone calls and weekend visits here and there. After Sam and Cody left last night, we stayed up watching old Disney movies again and then had chocolate chip pancakes this morning. Everything looked fine in the light, and I slept through most of the afternoon.

We're back on the sofa now with our takeout boxes, my feet draped over his knees like usual and my back against some flattened throw pillows.

"I'm glad to see you eating okay," Brent says. "I wasn't sure how much last night got to you."

I use a plastic knife to saw through the enchilada in my lap. I haven't thought about what happened with the scratching and the crickets since this morning. And maybe that's another mental health red flag, that I can *not* think about something like last night as soon as it's light again.

He rests a hand on my knee. "You *are* okay, aren't you?"

I nod. "It's just that I swore I heard those noises."

Brent holds my eyes for a second before looking down at his tacos. "But you're better now," he says.

"Sure." It's dark again, but of course I don't hear things with him on the sofa next to me. "Is your mom okay?" I ask, to change the subject.

He shrugs. "Think it's probably just a cold. She just doesn't wanna give it to you before the funeral. The dinner, I mean."

I try another bite of enchilada with a bunch of sauce, and heat prickles the roof of my mouth. I think Paco's must add the same peppers to this sauce as they do to the white cheese we used to gorge on together in middle school when Bev and my dad were out taking my mom to her treatments.

We talk about Dad's thing for a while between bites. Brent asks what I'll wear and what I still need to do before Friday, things like calling the caterer to give them a final payment and avoiding Becky Lange. Maybe celebrations of life are all like this, though— simple, after you're done the grieving. Maybe this time's like the daylight after new moons and long nights, when everything looks normal again.

Cody calls my cell phone when we're in the middle of a home renovation show Brent taped last night, and I get up and walk to my old bedroom to get away from the noise of the TV.

"I just wanted to see if you're doin' okay," Cody says when I answer.

I apologize again for last night and thank him for coming over.

"You're feelin' all right?"

"No problems tonight," I tell him, and almost add a *so far*. Sometimes, I think they're always right around the corner. But my watch hasn't recorded any extra steps, and my groceries haven't started disappearing or anything, so at least I'm not going anywhere or eating without knowing it.

"It must have been a panic attack," I tell him. "I'm sorry, and I really appreciate..."

"No," he says. "If it happens again, call, okay?"

I thank him, and we hang up.

Brent's looking at me when I come back to the living room. He's paused the show. "Who was that?" he asks.

I sit down, but he doesn't pull my feet up yet. My side of the sofa feels strange like this, with the cushion sloping down towards the middle.

"Cody Muller."

"That's weird," he says.

I reach for the quilt draped over the back of the sofa. "He was just checking on me after last night."

Brent doesn't say anything as he sets his plate down on the side table.

"What?" I ask.

He shakes his head. "It's just a little convenient, isn't it? That he was right next door?"

"He's redoing the Leeson's conservatory."

Brent doesn't respond. He eventually unpauses the house show, and I think about Cody through the big renovation reveal. This is the kind of thing he does for work, I think, but I can't really picture him on a show like this, full of dramatic roadblocks and tears when the family finally comes home.

When it goes to commercial, I turn back to Brent. I'm still sitting sideways, sinking into the middle of the sofa. "You don't trust Cody or what?"

He reaches for his drink. "Well, he was always kind of trouble, wasn't he?"

"I didn't really know him."

Brent shrugs. "Just be careful, okay?"

I agree, and then he picks up my feet again and sets them over his knees like usual.

I wake up sometime in the middle of *Saturday Night Live* with my head on Brent's shoulder and my feet curled up under the quilt. It reminds me of Saturday nights before, of falling asleep on sofas after summer floats or waffle cones from Wilson's ice cream barn out past the junction. Bev always had some pie baked for us in the colder months, plates made up and ready to zap in the microwave.

The TV volume's low, but I can't hear anything else over it tonight, any crickets or scratching or the other noises in my head. Brent has an arm behind me, and when I sit up and look at him in the glow of the TV, I think something's wrong on his face.

It's not until I feel his breath on my nose, though, that I think he might kiss me. This is something we don't do on Saturday nights, something we've never done before. Something I've never even thought about. I don't think he has, either.

I freeze. Then I guess we both snap out of it, back to ourselves. I flip the blanket over my feet, and he turns up the volume in time for the last SNL skit.

*     *

I'm thinking about Brent Monday morning as I eat my cereal. He didn't come over last night and didn't text me on his way into work this morning. I tell myself this would be normal any other time; it's not like we've spent the last decade talking at every meal, or even every day. It should feel normal now.

I wait for my fitness watch's app to sync with my phone. When the graph loads, it tells me I got almost eight hours of sleep, and I wonder if this is right, if I can still be normal, too. The house was quiet last night, and I left the TV on the *Golden Girls* channel in case I woke up.

I click through the step counter, then go to the heart rate chart. I zoom in on Saturday night, when there was a big spike. It was a temporary one, though, with Brent's face so close to mine. I want to think if I watch these things that I can control them, that this little dot out of line with the others was just a moment of panic like the crickets were.

I get a yellow notepad from the phone nook—one of my mom's, left in her drawer—and make a to-do list for the week to focus on something else. I tell myself the dinner thing would be stressful no matter what was going on with Brent or anything else.

My first chore's calling the caterer, Hart's.

A woman named Claudia I think is from Felden picks up, and I confirm the time and tell her I need to make a final payment.

"And you definitely want the beans," she says. "Not the green bean casserole?"

"Right." The casserole's a Paige dish I swear I can still taste from all the weddings and funerals I used to go to here. I must have had a few dozen pounds of Hart's green bean casserole smothered in cheddar through my childhood.

"That's it, then," Claudia says. "You're all set."

"You have my credit card?"

"Already taken care of."

I set down the notepad. I can feel my pulse picking up without having to check my watch. "Who?" I ask.

"The Rolenfelds."

I almost ask *why*, but of course Claudia's ahead of me.

"Your daddy did a great service to this community," she reminds me. "'s only right the Rolenfelds would want to honor that."

# 39



A couple minutes after Baer gets in on Monday morning, I'm holding a copy of the note from Kara's in front of his face. This is all I can do to pressure him to get a handwriting analysis, just standing here and trying to make him uncomfortable. Luckily, my standing here is all it takes to make him uncomfortable.

He takes the paper from me this time and sets it on his desk. "I'm not sayin' it's not real," he says. He's trying to sound like Sheriff Stan, I think, working on his drawl. All the guys here slip in and out of it when they remember.

I wait.

"But that's lot a money to be throwin' at somethin' that might not come back with any answers, and it's not been done here before, and I don't even know who we'd go to for that kinda..."

"I know a lab in Cincinnati that could do it overnight. We just have to scan it."

Baer looks at my badge. That's what he does now when he doesn't want to meet my eyes. "Sounds expensive," he says after a second.

"It's not."

Baer turns to his window then, to the traffic slowing down out on 31. It's almost lunchtime. "Say we did it," he says. "What would we even have to compare to it? What could we send 'em? Nothing we have a warrant for, I can tell you that much."

"It could give us a lead." Because that's what we do, in these cases, all we can do. Collect leads. Follow them. "We can send along a sample of Dalton's writing's that's public. He has something handwritten on his website, some civics lesson from when he was in school his people uploaded there. And we have the other note to compare."

"Samantha," Baer says, leaning back in his chair and heaving a deeper sigh. His uniform pulls tight across his stomach. "I don't wanna disappoint you, but you know this case has been closed for years." He thinks that's a thing from watching TV dramas, I think, that cases open and close like this. I guess he doesn't know how all those episodes end.

"And now it's open again," I tell him. "New evidence is being delivered. Literally delivered, right to Kara Peterson's doorstep."

"Okay." He blows out some air and looks down at his desk. "I can say somethin' to the night shift about goin' by there some more, but I don't know there's any real threat."

I point to the paper in front of him. "That one," I say. "That's a written threat."

He looks at it, still avoiding my eyes. "Or she wrote it herself because she was pissed off Dalton won the race and wanted some attention. Same as with that picture. She wasn't even in it. And the note from before. We don't know. There's no way *to* know. And she obviously can't pin this one on Dalton, with him at the party."

I wait until Baer's looking at me again. He always does, if I'm quiet for long enough. "I believe someone was there," I say.

"Where?"

I almost roll my eyes. But I've practiced not rolling my eyes so much, they tense up and don't do it even when I want them to now. I take a breath. "At Kara's house."

"Nothin' taken, though?"

I don't respond. Baer wouldn't know what's taken from these women if it bit him in the ass.

"So why'd you think somebody would do that?" he asks. He's slipping out of his Southern vowels now. "Why do you think Dalton, or anybody else, for that matter..." His face is that ruddy pink it gets when he's worked himself up.

"To terrorize her. To make her feel unsafe."

"Okay," he says, after a second. "So we send somebody by Peterson's to ask some questions, to write up a report and look into..."

"Kara's," I correct, "and I already did that."

There's a pause. Baer's part of this town's old guard, but he was handpicked by Kara's father, mentored by him. So you'd think he'd care about at least this case a little more.

He taps a pen on his desk for a minute, what he does when he's thinking. "I understand, you know," he says, "why this case might get your attention."

I meet his eyes, challenge him to say something else.

He shrugs and looks away. "But you have to understand—and I know you're from the city, probably not used to how we do things here yet—things are just a little different out here."

"We have someone being threatened. And you didn't even run her rape kit." I got the samples back from Lisa this morning and put them in Kara's box again before the guys got in. No one noticed anything was missing.

Baer stiffens and flushes a deeper pink. "That was Stan's decision," he says.

"Even though Kara's his daughter?"

"*Especially* with her bein' his daughter." He puts his pen down. "Look, you know I care about this, too. But this town, you've got to understand, it's like an ecosystem. You go badmouthing the Rolenfelds or throw somethin' old like that into question, and everything goes off balance. *Everything.*"

"I understand," I tell him, and smile like I've practiced before I go. And I do understand. I'll do it myself.

Stubsen's waiting at my desk when I come out of Baer's office. He doesn't have a pretense this time.

"Everything okay in there?" he asks.

"Fine."

"It's not Kara Peterson again, is it?"

I shrug and pull out my chair. It's supposed to look like relief when you shrug, like letting go. Stubsen wouldn't know shoulders lifting is really the opposite.

"Not anymore," I tell him. "I guess I was barking up the

wrong tree."

Stubsen nods, exhales, lets his shoulders down a little. "We all do that sometimes," he says. "Hey, if you want, I could take you to the funeral."

"Funeral?"

He walks around to his corner of my desk. "For Stan. I know you only met him the once, but..."

"The dinner thing?"

"Yeah. It's, you know, since they didn't have a regular funeral..."

"Yes," I say, and force another smile. "I'd like that."

# 40

*Kara*

The days before my dad's dinner pass quickly with storms that leave a carpet of soggy leaves over the woods. The pressure changes always give me a headache, or at least I tell myself that's all it is, something about pressure and Paige that my fitness watch can't track.

I haven't seen Brent since Saturday night, we both say because we're catching up on work, him with all the extra HR training that's been keeping him late at the factory and me because I can always say this. No one here knows my schedule.

I used to think things between us would be the same forever, but it's like we don't know each other the way we used to when he comes over as I'm getting ready late Friday afternoon.

"I brought another pie," he says as the screen door snaps shut behind him. He's wearing the navy suit he's had since Bree Leeson's wedding, when he had to half carry me back down the aisle with a broken heel.

I look behind him, for Bev.

"Mom's sorry she can't make it. But it's pumpkin, your

favorite."

"She's still sick?"

He nods and opens the refrigerator.

"You don't still think it's just a cold, then."

He moves around a couple milks to fit the pie on the middle shelf, denting the tin foil when he pushes it back. "You know Mom," he says. "I don't know if it's an early flu or what, but she always says it's gonna pass soon. I only know it's bad cause she isn't here for this."

"Sure," I say, and make a mental note to call her tomorrow. The only time I remember Bev missing anything was for those couple months after her accident, when Brent came to stay with us while she healed. I guess that's how all this got started, whatever we are now.

"You look good," he says, following me to my old bedroom.

I mumble a thank you that doesn't sound right as I look for the ankle boots I picked out before. When I don't find them in my closet, I grab the black kitten heels I wore to the gala, instead. I should probably be more dressed up anyway.

"Really," Brent tells me. "You look good."

I thank him again, but I look like I've lost weight. These pants don't fit as snug around my hips anymore, and the black sweater I just got in August hangs on me. I'd usually make a joke about this, or Brent would. But maybe we're too old to make jokes about our bodies anymore.

I open the door to my bathroom and stand a few paces back from the full length mirror there. When Brent comes around behind me, I pretend to adjust my top as I study our reflection. Do we look right together, I wonder? Right in a different way, I mean, than we used to. I can't tell. I guess it's because I've seen us together so many times that we always look just normal to me.

"The slideshow turned out nice," he says. "I think you'll like it."

I trip as I hurry past him back through the doorway. I'd almost forgotten about the slideshow, about all the pictures he put together of my dad, all the work he's done for this over the last few months. Brent took over so many things like that when I didn't come home right away.

"Thanks," I tell him. "I really appreciate that."

"It's no problem." He looks at the door, then back at me. "I guess we should get going," he says.

I follow him out through the kitchen and scrape the damp leaves from my heels before I climb into his truck.

When we get to the old rec room at the church, what used to be my elementary school's cafeteria, it's these memories, not the ones of my dad, that come flooding back. I think of those little, multi-colored chairs pushed into long tables and the double lines where the lunch ladies served us square pizzas and hot browns and mashed potatoes.

Tonight, the clatter's different, full of older voices, and the place doesn't look the same with round tables draped in tablecloths and lined with maroon-cushioned chairs. But it still doesn't seem like a funeral. Maybe it's because we're calling it something different, or because I put it off for so long.

I stand at the wall that backs to the new bathrooms, like Becky Lange directs me to, away from the buffet carts guys from Hart's are stocking now by the kitchen. Brent's slideshow plays on a projector screen behind me.

A line forms quickly, the first people coming inside a little over half an hour before we're supposed to start, and this demands enough of my attention, these phrases I've said probably hundreds of times in lines like these, to keep me from thinking too much. It's funny how you can listen to so many stories about someone without any memories coming back, how you can grieve without really being present.

People here know this routine. They move in circles around the room, hugging me before going to the buffet, settling down to eat, making their way to the dessert table Becky's put a bunch of mums around, and then waving a goodbye before they leave.

As the evening goes on, it starts to feel like Brent and I are back to normal, too, back to a routine. He stays by my side with tissues I haven't needed yet and a little plate of finger foods he tries to get me to take bites from every few minutes. Bev must have told him to keep me eating.

The place stays loud, voices bouncing off the concrete walls as people tell me stories about my dad. It's like the whole county knew him. Better than I did, obviously.

Three older men are in front of me now, all a little tipsy. One leans forward, breathing into my face. "And there was that one—you remember, don't cha, Doug? He tells it better than I do, anyway—in Columbus, at that strip club for Kline's birthday, that..."

He stops himself, or one of the other guys does, before he can finish the story. Brent takes over this group then, laughs and claps one of them on the back before turning them towards the buffet. When they're gone, my first grade teacher steps up and gives me a hug.

The line just keeps going like this—one hug, one story after another. I can't see the clock and don't know how much time's passing.

I don't start paying attention again until I see a little crowd forming over by the ramp to the parking lot and catch a glimpse of Robert Rolenfeld.

Brent leans closer. "It'll be okay," he whispers.

I nod and keep my smile. But suddenly, this is when it hits me, when the tears push up behind my eyes—not thinking about my dad, how I should be tonight, and not even because of all these stories that sound like someone I don't remember. Maybe it's that I should know them, the sudden realization I'm an outsider in my old cafeteria. It shouldn't be such a production for me to smile at Robert Rolenfeld, at least as a neighbor; if things had gone how I wanted, I would have been in Paige for a while now, a real member of this community.

I keep an eye on Rolenfeld as the line brings him closer. I talk to a cop from Dale who went to training with Dad back in the day and nod as he echoes that line they must have written in the obituary about him being the best sheriff Ohio's ever seen, and then I listen to a lady who works at Gleson's and tells me about Dad eating all their about-to-expire Peeps one year.

"Rolenfeld won't make a scene," Brent says when there's a quiet moment between people. "All you have to do is shake his hand."

I nod, but I'm pretty sure that's all the Rolenfelds do, make scenes.

My high school principal hugs me, and then I notice Kym Hartmann step out of line when she gets close. She beelines for the little bar area at the back, not looking at me.

"She's pissed at you?" I ask Brent. Because you don't just get out of a Paige funeral line.

"Don't worry about it," he says.

"Something new?" I ask, wanting this distraction, to think about anything but Rolenfeld getting closer.

"It's about her intern. She's just jealous."

Then Cody Muller's in front of us. He looks from me to Brent, and I'm not sure for a second if he's going to hug me like the others have. He reaches out and shakes my hand, instead.

"You're doin' great," he tells me. "And this is a really nice night. Stan would have liked that it's a party."

I thank him and notice he's looking at Brent again when he goes to join Sam in the middle of the room.

# 41



*Sam*

Rolenfeld has his own orbit of guests circling him by the time Stubsen points him out to me. It's the first time I've seen him in person, but he looks just like he does on TV, in a pricey pinstripe suit with a smile that doesn't touch the rest of his face.

Stubsen goes right to him, fawning like the others, as I greet Cody and creep closer to the front of the line so I can hear better. At least Dalton's not with him. I get the impression Robert's more stable. He's had to be, I guess, has had to put on this public face for decades now.

Everyone seems to go quiet when he gets to Kara, and then he makes a good show of taking her hand and talking louder than he needs to. He tells her what an extraordinary man Stan was, a true hero in the community. It's rehearsed, not genuine, but at least it's not a threat.

Kara lets him hold her hand. She's just barely rocking back and forth on her heels, but she gets through it like she has everything else.

Later, once Rolenfeld's gone, Stubsen comes back, and we

stick around to talk to some cops a district over in the corner behind the dessert table. They tell Sheriff Stan stories, too, but all the ones I know already, or at least the ones I expect. None of them give me anything new. I guess I don't know quite what I'm listening for, though. It's not like they're going to say anything about who *didn't* love him at his funeral, about anyone who might have wanted him dead.

Stubsen lays a hand on my back as we cross the floor to leave, putting on his own show, and I focus on the door and the wind that stings my cheeks when we get out to the parking lot.

"So you and Stan," I say as soon as we're in his SUV. "You must have been close." But he hasn't teared up today or anything. None of them have.

Stubsen nods. "Stan was close with all us guys. 's just the kind of boss he was."

"Sure," I say, "but you spent a lot of time with him, didn't you? And you've been on the force for a long time. You must have known him better than the others."

"The best there was, if you ask me."

"Of course." I try to find the right words, to make this light, but I botch the transition. "Is he the one who got you hooked on coffee?"

Stubsen's face doesn't change. "Nah. Been drinkin' that since high school."

"As much as you do now?"

He smiles, glances over at me. "You've been payin' attention," he says.

I wait.

"Doesn't keep me up or anything."

"Sure," I say. "The other guys, too?"

"Yeah. You're the only one who's a tea drinker 'round here." He turns to me again when we get to the light at St. Luke's, and I wonder if he thinks this is flirting.

"And that powder stuff you put in it," I say. "What's that?"

"Oh, that's just an extra boost, some vitamins. You wanna try it? I've got one in chocolate flavor at home I can bring..."

"That's okay," I interrupt. "You said it's what killed Stan, though, didn't you? The coffee," I add quickly.

It's quiet for a second as we pull onto 31. "Probably," Stubsen says then, and I realize I've been holding my breath. "He had high blood pressure, I think."

"For how long?"

"Wouldn't know. Why?"

"My dad had that," I tell him. "I always worry about it."

"You probably don't have to worry," Stubsen says. "Cause you're so skinny, you know." He thinks this is a compliment.

When we get to the station—I told him I needed to work on some paperwork so he didn't come get me at the house—I hop down from his SUV and thank him for the ride.

"You got plans for the rest of the weekend?" he asks.

I tell him I'm working again tomorrow before I hurry inside. I watch from the window as he drives away, then go out to my car.

# 42

*Kara*

It's late when Brent finally drives me home, and the woods are dark when we get in. I hit the switch for the floodlights along the back of the house, sending a flash out into the trees.

"You did really good," Brent tells me when I thank him again.

I hang up my coat in the hall closet and kick off my shoes. My feet hurt, but at least there aren't any blisters. I haven't worn heels for so many years, and I was standing for a while.

Brent wraps me in a hug when I turn around. We stay there for just a second too long.

"What's that for?" I ask when we pull away.

"Tonight was hard. You want me to heat up some of that pie for you?"

"You have some," I tell him, emptying my little clutch purse back into my usual bag. "I think I just need a shower and to go to bed."

"You want me to stay?"

I don't look at him now. I want to say it's because he seems off tonight, but maybe it's because he'll notice, if he stays too long, because he'll see something's wrong with me. I could lose more lights or lotions or something worse, something bigger. So maybe it doesn't have anything to do with Brent at all.

I plug in my phone on the counter. "Thanks," I tell him. "I think I'm okay."

He doesn't respond for a second. "All right," he says, then, "I should catch up on some stuff anyway. I was thinking of going to Columbus tomorrow night for that concert."

"Concert?"

"The one I told you about. Leah got tickets for us."

"Leah..."

"Schulz. Kym's intern."

"Right," I say, "of course. I remember."

He says something about a new dinner place in downtown Columbus as I follow him to the door.

"You're sure this is what you want?" he asks when he turns back to me. "I can stay, you know."

I tell him I'm okay, and he leaves without giving me another hug. I stay at the window and watch him get in his truck and drive back to Bev's.

# 43



*Sam*

Stubsen's doing his gargoyle impression on my desk Saturday morning. I like this predictability about him. It makes me feel more secure, at least gives me the illusion that I understand him, that I know what he could do.

He's made my tea this time, or at least what he thinks is my tea. He doesn't know about the honey.

"Seems like you're workin' really hard," he says. "Not the Peterson case again, though, is it?"

"No," I tell him, "just paperwork this weekend. But I have been thinking about that."

He leans forward, rests an arm on my computer tower.

I look around the room. The others are several feet away, still loitering in the kitchen. "I'm worried about Dalton," I say.

Stubsen frowns. "Cause of Kara, or..."

"Not Kara."

He doesn't say anything for a second.

"I've just been thinking about whether there's enough security around the Rolenfelds. I know Dalton's pretty young to be in congress, and I'm worried this is a new time for political rivalries, and with the way people like to stir up trouble…"

It's Sheriff Stan's phrase, of course, that gets his attention. Peterson must have said it ten times during my interview.

"You think Dalton's in danger?" Stubsen asks.

"I think people in the public eye like him should always be a little extra careful. Don't you?"

"Course," he says.

"Do they have cameras around the property?"

He nods. "Infrared. The best. He's got 'em all the way around the house."

"But what about the woods? What if someone came around the back? It wouldn't be hard to get a shot at a window, would it? I drove by the other day, and there are so many windows…"

Stubsen's still nodding. "You're right," he says. "I'll say something to him about it. Thanks a lot."

I swirl my tea and wait.

"You don't think there's somebody in particular…"

"Not necessarily. It's just that I've been thinking about Kara's report at the hospital, that someone else was there that night. It's not that I don't believe you about Dalton, but what about somebody else? What if there was another person involved?"

"Somebody else," Stubsen echoes.

"Well, if there was someone else in the room, that leaves Dalton as the only witness."

Stubsen doesn't move, and I study his face.

"Whoever *that* was, they'd have a good reason to keep Dalton quiet," I prompt.

"Yeah," Stubsen says, finally. "Yeah. That's right. You're right. I'll talk to him about it. Thanks."

"Absolutely." I take a sip of my tea.

"You busy tonight?" he asks.

"Facetime date with my family," I tell him. "They're having a kind of reunion."

His smile sticks in the corners of his lips. "Great," he says. "That's great."

# 44

*Kara*

Saturday night, I try to think about anything but Brent in Columbus with his work friends. This should be easy; we've had more Saturday nights apart than together in the last decade, and I've never thought about them before.

I play some music on my phone and keep myself busy sorting through my dad's old work room. I'd forgotten it until now. It's funny, I think, how you can forget things when they're just barely out of sight. This building's probably one of the bigger selling points of the house, too. I bet Becky Lange will call it a future rental opportunity, but it's really just an insulated garage with bits of wood and sawdust covering most of the concrete. Maybe someone will turn it into a guest cottage or a she shed or something down the road like they do on the house channel.

The space reminds me of Dad more than anything at his dinner did. It must be something about being here in his dust, around all these things he left unfinished. He started coming here after Mom died, converted it from whatever it was before and made it his own. His radio's plugged in on the floor in a corner still, the one with the volume knob that pops off. I remember trying to twist around the little rod with my fingers and yelling at him over the buzz of the machines when I'd get home from school.

The space reminds me a little of Baer, too. He used to come over on Sunday afternoons, and I'd always marvel at how their friendship could hang together the way it did when neither of them could ever hear anything the other said. But maybe male relationships are cemented by sanding things, just being in the same place together, like handshakes at St. Mark's and haircuts at Nancy's and coffees at The Strawberry.

I can't tell what all the wood pieces and tools scattered around the room are, if they're scraps or parts of something bigger, so I tackle just the shelves tonight—boxes of old taxes, mainly, and other things that need to be shredded. I never did Dad's taxes. He was so comfortable with his old guy on the square.

I have a couple bags full of papers for the shredder by the time my phone beeps to say it's low on battery. The last time I checked, it was after ten; maybe I've been focused on this for too long.

I'm afraid I'll hear things when I unplug the radio and head back to the house, but it's quiet tonight. There aren't any crickets. I take a breath before I turn off the lights, and then it takes a second for my eyes to adjust once I've closed the door behind me.

# 45

Cody Muller's waiting in his truck with his headlights off, watching Kara's place. He's about to go back to the Leeson's when he sees it—a shadow creeping along the edge of the house, right around the bathroom where Kara heard the scratching.

He doesn't hesitate then, doesn't bother to grab anything or shut the door to his truck behind him. He sprints between the trees, the leaves damp and quiet and his boots barely sucking down into the mud.

He loses sight of the shadow for a couple seconds. Then it appears just a few feet in front of him.

He tackles it, reaching out in the darkness and landing with a soft *thud* on the ground.

# 46

*Kara*

It's like my heart won't go back to normal now, like maybe nothing will ever be normal again.

I look at Cody. He's standing on the other side of the kitchen island. My eyes go to his cheek, to the long scratch there. The scratch I made. Dark beads of blood are still coming out at the top. I thought it might need stitches, but he's said a few times that we shouldn't go to the ER. I know I'd argue with this any other night, but I can't think of what we'd tell the triage nurses or what it would sound like tomorrow once the story had spread through the churches and the whole town had repeated it and added their own takes.

Cody knew it was me as soon as we hit the ground, he said, and of course he stopped fighting right away, just let me roll on top of him and scratch up his face. I don't know why I didn't stop fighting, why it took me so long to realize he was yelling my name. He wasn't holding onto me or anything. I could have run. I thought I would have run. But I guess you don't always know what you'd do until it happens.

He turns away, pouring a mug of coffee for each of us. That's what he did when we got inside, before I could think of what to do—he put on the pot like he'd done it a thousand times, pulling over a couple mugs and changing the filter.

He's looking out the window again now, for something that's not there. I wasn't what he thought I was when he tackled me, he said, what he was sitting in his truck between my dad's place and the Leeson's looking for. It feels more like a *what* in my head, still, than a *who*, this monster that always makes me think it's outside. I don't tell him maybe he just saw the other version of me, who I am when I don't remember. She's crept through these woods at least once before.

"I think you'd better clean that out," he says.

I reach up and feel the scratch by my eye. I didn't know it was there until he told me. From a twig, I guess, when I hit the ground.

"I'm okay." I keep saying it.

He wets another paper towel and hands it to me across the island. There's a pile of these on the counter in front of me now, all pink with blood. Cody's stayed on that side of the island since we came in.

He leans back against the sink. "Tell me what I can do," he says.

I tell him I'm okay again, like I should be.

"You're shaking. It's gettin' cold out. Would it help to warm up? If you went and took a shower or somethin'?"

"No."

"Is it the window? In the shower?"

I want to tell him I'm not afraid of windows, that I've showered in both of these bathrooms with windows looking out into the woods and never been scared of them before.

"I will in the morning," I say instead.

"What about now?"

"Now?"

"What are you doin' now?" Cody asks, like maybe I have plans tonight. "Are you gonna go to sleep or…"

"No." That can wait until the morning, too, when the woods are light again. There's not enough moonlight tonight. I take a sip of my coffee. I still have adrenaline or whatever it is going through me, keeping my heart fast. "I guess I'll stay up, do some things around the house," I tell him. "I'm trying to get it ready."

He sets down his mug. "Good," he says. "I can help."

I open my mouth, and I think I'm about to say that he should go home, or at least back to Martha's, that I don't need someone here with me to feel safe. But these would just be more lies in the dark.

"Maybe you can tell me what to do," Cody says after a few seconds. "Maybe there are things that need to get fixed before you put it on the market."

I look around the kitchen. It seems like my brain's slow for how fast my heart is now.

He asks me some basic questions as I sip more of my coffee, like where the hot water system and the electrical panels are. It only takes me a few seconds to remember, and I set down the mug and lead him to the little closet under the stairs.

"I'm not sure about the stove," I say when I remember this.

Cody follows me back to the kitchen, but he stays several feet behind me. "Has it been actin' up, or..."

"I haven't tried it." Because I wanted to feel like this was temporary, I think, not like I was settling in to stay. I don't tell Cody this, though. He has enough reasons to think I'm crazy.

He goes around to the other side of the island and turns one of the knobs. It clicks a couple times before the flame catches.

"It looks like you'll need new filters for your air system and some little things like that," he says once he's turned off the stove. "Most everybody does. And a new circuit on the electrical panel to pass an inspection. And the balcony railing isn't too sturdy."

I look at the back windows.

"I saw it was warped when I went around the house," he says.

I nod. I don't want to tell him I haven't been out there. At least that I remember.

"Should be easy," he adds.

I try to say the right things as we walk through the rest of the rooms, ignoring what brought us here. Eventually, I get out the pumpkin pie Brent brought over yesterday and cut us each a piece like we're having some sort of normal get-together. Cody stays across the island from me as we eat.


I finally take a shower while Cody's messing with the garbage disposal and the night's fading into a lighter blue. He doesn't leave until I'm back downstairs with another mug of coffee and the sun's peeking through the trees.

# 47



*Sam*

Sunday morning, Cody's at my front door before I leave to meet him for brunch. I see right away something's wrong even though he's not fidgeting. It's the stiffness in his body, a hard kind of stillness. Cody's one of those rare people who don't have any tells in movement when there's something wrong, so it took me a while to get a baseline on him.

He ignores the tea I make him. I don't think he was paying attention when I asked if he wanted some.

"I don't understand," I say once he's stopped talking. This is the longest I've heard him talk. "You *tackled* her?"

He reaches for the screen door to the porch, frowning as he pushes the little lock on it up and down. He seems too big in this sitting room, with his head so close to the crown molding. "I thought it was somebody else," he says, still focused on the door.

"You were watching for..."

He looks back at me again. "After the funeral, when everybody knew she was home, I thought..."

These are the kinds of thoughts no one wants to finish. I look at his face. It's quiet, watching me. He thinks there's still something I'm missing. And he's right.

"You think you saw someone there," I say. "Someone else."

He rubs his temples. "Yeah. I thought so. I thought it was too big for her at first. But I lost track of him, and then it was her in front of me. I didn't know till we were on the ground."

I take a sip of my Earl Grey, cool now.

"She shouldn't be stayin' out there alone," Cody says.

I think of how I'd write this down, if it were a witness statement instead of Cody standing in my living room, what questions I'd ask him, what assumptions I'd try to avoid. I'd ask first if he thought Kara were in danger. Sometimes people who are closer to a case have better insights into what danger looks like. But of course he thinks she's in danger, or he wouldn't be here. And he wouldn't have been there, either, just waiting for something to happen.

He turns away from the door and paces back towards my kitchen. "What can we do?" he asks.

I focus on my tea, on the darker swirls of honey pooling at the bottom, as I tell him we've increased patrols on that side of town, instructing the guys on night shift to take some loops around the junction and to keep an eye out for anything suspicious. But I sound like Baer and hate myself for it.

Cody's stopped pacing and is looking at me when I set my mug back on the coffee table. Of course he hears it. These responses are never enough.

"There has to be somethin' you can do," he says. "This..."

I gesture for him to sit down. "Can you tell me about Stan?" I ask.

He doesn't move. "Stan? Why?"

I glance at the clock on the wall, an old cuckoo that came with the place. "Why don't we get pickup today," I say, because it looks like we could both use this, a good meal. And because this is a conversation I can't have in public.

"Fine," Cody says, but he doesn't sit.

"It's something with Stan's autopsy," I say after a few seconds. "There was a number that sort of jumped out. At my friend Lisa, anyway, in Cincinnati. You don't know this. I haven't told anyone at the station."

He nods, barely.

"I copied the coroner's report and sent it to her. It might not be anything, or connected to what's going on with Kara even if it *is* something."

Cody waits. He can be so damn still.

"Caffeine. A lot of it."

"From coffee?"

"Did Stan drink a lot of coffee?"

Cody looks down at the tea mug he still hasn't touched. "I guess so," he says.

"But it flagged, Lisa thought. There was enough that it should have been suspicious. It could have been something somebody put in his drink."

I try to focus on Cody, on his response, but I can't stop thinking about Stubsen and his white powder. Lisa said she could run that, too, could try to estimate how much Stan would have had to take to get to his blood level. Someone should have looked into it before now. Answers are always limited, always just estimates once the corpse is gone.

"Who did Stan have coffee with?" I ask. "Outside of the office?"

"Pretty much everybody in town, I guess."

"You, too?"

Cody nods. "At the Strawberry every now and then. But he was there with somebody about every time I went in."

"Different people?" A list of names probably wouldn't be worth anything; Stan was right in the middle of everything here like the pole at the center of a carousel.

"Yeah."

"And no enemies?" I ask. "You don't remember any contentious charges or anything like that? Anyone who might have held a grudge?"

Cody shakes his head and finally sits down on the loveseat. "No cases I know of. But this is Paige," he reminds me. "There are a heck of a lot of grudges."

# 48

*Kara*

I nap through most of the day Sunday. There aren't any traces of last night left over, and the woods are flooded with watery sunlight with just a few clouds rolling in from out past the junction.

When I finally get out of bed, I decide to focus on clearing out my old bedroom closet. It's important to keep doing things, I think, to keep my mind occupied.

My closet's just how I left it after rummaging around for something to wear to the gala—sweaters for Christmas break the last time I was home still hanging at the front and accessories piling up where I used to get dressed in the middle.

The back's like a museum of my childhood. I set aside the big blue box with my First Communion dress—we wrap them up, here, like wedding dresses—and fish out a stray neon headband from behind it. On the other side, my senior prom dress is cocooned in so many layers of plastic it looks like some kind of oversized pink larvae. As I unwrap it and run my fingers over the tulle, I remember buying it, but I don't have any memory of what it felt like on.

I think of how I walked right by this one when I first went dress shopping with Bev. I went back to the mall and got it later to appease my dad, because he thought the other sent the wrong message. So I ended up in this pink tulle A-line covered in little beads with a square neckline right at my collarbone that he said made me look like a princess.

I must have thought I was the only senior at prom, except maybe Kym Hartmann, who looked like a fairy tale princess and not an eighteen year old woman, but I can't remember how I reacted, if I sulked or complained or quietly stuffed the bra with those little pads they sell at Carson's and made the best of it. There should be a wrap somewhere that I put over my shoulders for pictures here at the house and ditched as soon as we got to the gym.

I remember the rest of prom better—Parker Lange's dress, a backless, bright yellow satin with a slit up to her spanks she had to tug at all night. And the pale blue strapless one of Amy Schmitt's with the sequins on top, and the way Matt Roberts' white tux glowed under the black light on the dance floor.

Behind a pile of purses, there's a shoebox full of prom pictures. I'm smiling in all of them, not looking like me. But I guess you never do, with the heavy makeup and that giant curl all us Paige girls had right at the front of our updos. I take a picture with my phone of one with me and Brent. We're standing under an arch covered in fake roses, in an awkward pose like you do, my hand on his chest and his on my hip.

I text it to him, and there's a little "read" check mark by it a few minutes later, but he still hasn't responded by the time I have a garbage bag full of clothes for St. Vinny's. As I'm going through my underwear drawer, I find some polaroids from back when his dad was still alive—both of our families posing outside St. Mark's after our kindergarten Christmas pageant and having a picnic on one of our vacations to the lake.

I don't take a picture of any of these. I'm not sure Brent will want to see them. He was younger when his dad died than I was with Mom, and he couldn't really talk about it then, either. So I text him instead about the concert in Columbus, like I'm just thinking about it now.

Any other time, I'm sure I'd have told him about what happened last night right away. But I guess I'm doing the same thing he did with his dad, wanting to push it behind me. It's like if I keep pushing these things behind me, eventually, I'll outpace them.

There's still no response an hour later, and I set the polaroids out on the kitchen counter so I'll remember to take them over to Bev.


My prom dress and the too-short black one are on top of a giant giveaway pile at the edge of my bed, and I'm taking a bag of trash—the little things that just build up over the years—down to the garage when my phone buzzes on the dresser.

*Is it a good time to stop by?* I assume it's Brent at first, but it's Cody. It should have been Brent, I think. He's usually so quick texting back.

*Great,* I tell Cody.

I don't notice the darkness outside the windows until I get downstairs. I wonder why it doesn't hit me all the time, why some nights are so quiet.

The coffee's almost finished brewing by the time Cody comes over. He greets me and asks how everything's going, walking straight to the other side of the kitchen as soon as he's taken off his boots. I think of this as his spot, after last night, with the big granite island between us.

He sets down a canvas bag with some tools and says he has a couple things to show me. I nod along and try to look like I understand, like I'm an adult who owns a house and makes her own decisions.

"I'll have to bring that circuit by later for the electric," he says, "but this is the best kinda filter for an older HVAC, and I've got a new float for the toilet."

"The toilet?"

"The one that keeps runnin' down the hall."

Of course that's when I remember it, when I can hear it again. I guess it's been background noise for too long. It's funny how it wasn't louder, I think, like everything else was that night with the scratching and the crickets. I don't remember the water at all.

I thank Cody and pour out a couple mugs of coffee. He drinks his black, or maybe he just didn't want to look for sugar or cream last night. He's only seen me in black coffee mode, too. He probably assumes this is how I am all the time, how I've always been.

I try to say things that sound normal, to talk to him like we've known each other for as long as we should have and like I'm someone who can talk to men.

"You were on the football team, weren't you?" I ask when he's kneeling in front of a vent I hadn't noticed before under the staircase.

"Yeah," he says. "A year behind you."

"Right." I think of how little Brent and I interacted with anyone else in high school. We wouldn't have fit in with the jocks like Cody or the band kids or any of the others. Or maybe we would have, if it hadn't been just us for so long by then.

I don't know what to ask Cody about football, so I ask him about construction, instead, and about starting his own business.

He works quickly, moving onto the next vent and taking out another filter blackened with dust. He tells me a little about what he does, but only the things I ask, and I don't know the right questions.

When he heads to the powder room, I ask if I could learn these things he's doing—not the complicated stuff like with the electric panel, but maybe just a filter or something.

He holds out the toilet part to me, a white plastic dish like the milk carton bird bath I made in Mrs. Henke's class in first grade.

"Would you show me?" I ask. "I have a toilet back at home..." I stop, laugh. I didn't think I'd laugh tonight. Maybe it's that there aren't any windows in this hallway, or maybe I feel safer when someone else is here.

Cody's smiling when I look back at him, and he tells me about the float and what it does, relative to all the other toilet parts I don't know. My dad always took care of these things. It made me think this kind of work was only for people who made things with saws or who played football or worked on building crews, just like changing the oil in my car or checking the tire pressure. Dad did that every time I drove home from college. It was how he showed affection, Bev always told me, checking my tire pressure and telling me the numbers, because he didn't know what else to talk to me about.

Cody lifts the lid off the tank at the back of the toilet, and then I have no idea what I'm looking at. He stands behind me and points out the parts, unscrewing the old float when I can't get my fingers around the joint. I feel like he's close to me, and he's so much taller, but there are a couple feet between his torso and mine even when he's bending over the tank. The rest of the time, he stays on the other side of the sink.

Once I've gotten the new float on, the toilet flushes, and the water goes quiet as soon as the reservoir's filled back up. I don't know why this flush feels so good to me, like I imagine passing the bar would have. Maybe I've just felt bad at everything for too long.

I thank Cody, and we go back to the kitchen and talk about the railing on my old balcony and how the humidity affects the boards for the couple minutes it takes him to finish his coffee.

"I'll come by to work on the circuit box later this week," he says, "if it's okay."

I start to protest, to say he doesn't have to do this and try to pay him for today, but he waves me off.

"I'm gonna be next door the rest of the night. So call if anything comes up, okay? Even if you don't think it's anything."

"You're working all night?"

He washes out his mug, his back to me. "I like to work when it's quiet," he says. "There are trades in during the days, and I can get more done this way. And Martha asked me to stay over when I could. You know her plants. She likes me to talk to 'em."

I nod and feel my shoulders relax, thinking of Cody being right next door telling Martha's fig trees and amaryllis about how toilets work and why you should change HVAC filters every few months.

"Can I get you some food or something?" I ask. "I have more pie from Bev."

"I'm good," he says, bending to tie his boots. "But maybe a favor?"

"Sure."

He's quiet for a second. "Maybe don't say anything about this to Brent?"

"Brent?"

Cody doesn't look at me as he straightens and pulls on his jacket. "With me comin' over. Guys get…weird, you know, about that kinda thing sometimes."

"Of course," I say, though I'm not sure I do know this.

I turn on the floodlights when he goes outside and watch him pull out of Brent's usual spot.

# 49



Monday morning, Stubsen's perched on the corner of my desk a little before nine. I've cleared some more room behind the computer tower so he doesn't slide off as easily now.

"On the forty-five," he says, trying to catch my eye.

I look at my computer screen, then back at him. I wasn't paying attention to the beginning of this. I've been trying to think of how to bring up Stan Peterson again.

"It's gonna be great. The game," Stubsen prompts.

Right. Football, Friday. He's started on the weekend early this week. "In Columbus?" I ask.

His forehead crinkles for just a second as I try to remember if I ever told him I liked football.

"That's great," I add.

So he keeps talking about how I can have Wagner's ticket if I want it—he really ought to spend some time with his kids this weekend, anyway—and about a new sports bar downtown.

"Shoot, *this* Friday?" I ask.

"Yeah."

"Sorry, I thought you were talking about *next* Friday," I tell him. "I'm catching up with a friend in Cincinnati this weekend."

Stubsen frowns. "Friend?"

"I've told you about Lisa, haven't I?"

"Oh," he says. "Lisa. Yeah. Well, that's too bad. So you goin' out or what?"

"Just a girls night." I don't have a segue, so I pretend I'm just now seeing his coffee mug. "Hey, I've been thinking about trying your energy powder."

"Yeah?"

"Maybe," I say. "Do you know the ingredients? I'm allergic to some sweeteners."

He hops off the desk and goes for the bottle. When he hands it over, I pretend to study the label until some of the other guys get in and he's called over to the kitchen.

I wait until his back's to me, then dump a scoop of the powder into the plastic bag in my purse. I added milk to my tea already, and it looks just like the powder makes all the guys' coffees look, creamy and thick.

"You like it?" Stubsen asks when he comes back a few minutes later. "Didn't know if you're a French vanilla girl or not."

I raise the milky tea to my lips and take a sip.

"Perfect," I tell him.


That night, my rounds take me all the way out to the junction, or at least they could.

There's a new security camera on the floor of my passenger seat. I paired it with my computer as soon as it came yesterday, in a browser with a VPN. So no one will be able to find my home IP address even if they somehow find the camera. It's one of the infrared ones that work on solar and satellite transmissions so you don't have to set them up with power or wifi. All the things Stubsen knew.

I walk around the Leeson's place, where Cody's been working, careful not to step on anything that might be dormant in Martha's gardens. Cody's in Dale now picking up some supplies. He'll bring pizza on his way back from the place in Felden, and maybe then we'll eat out on the patio he glassed in earlier this fall, where Martha first invited me over for some sweet tea and shortbread cookies with raspberry jam in the August heat.

This little path between the trees is the easiest way to get to Kara's house on foot, and I stop at a big evergreen right in the middle of a clump of oaks that have already lost most of their leaves.

The little solar panel hides easily in the needles of the lower branches. I've already put tape over the red dot that blinks when it's recording something, and I'm back at Martha's waiting for Cody twenty minutes before he pulls into the drive.

# 50

*Kara*

Tuesday afternoon, the house is almost out of piles to be sorted. I'm out of work at the firm, too. It's weird how quickly work goes when I'm here, when I want it to take longer, but maybe there's something to that, why Paige is so industrious, known for all its hard workers and people like the Rolenfelds who say they care about them.

Everything I still need to get rid of is my dad's. I haven't really talked to anyone since the funeral, and I'll have to soon to know what to do with some of his things. I keep forgetting to ask Cody about the stuff in the workshop.

My cell phone buzzes just as I'm getting out a frozen lasagna.

It's Brent, finally. *I'm okay*, he says, *just busy*. And of course he *should* be busy, I think, with work and with everything that was in his life before I came back to town. So maybe everything really is normal between us.

*I'll come by tomorrow?* he asks.

*Great. Are you home?* I ask.

*Out tonight. Staying here.*

At the loft, he means. So I put off lunch, or dinner, or whatever it is—I'm not that hungry, anyway—tossing the lasagna back into the freezer and grabbing the polaroids to take over to Bev since she's alone now.

The sun's low in the trees when I get outside, the breeze harder than I thought, and I decide to come home before it's fully dark out. It's funny, though, how I've always felt safer outside, even at night. It's the quiet inside that gets me.

The ground between our places is mushy and covered in soggy leaves. Bev doesn't answer the door right away, and I almost turn the handle and go in like I used to. But I wait this time.

There's some noise from the kitchen, and when Bev gets to the window, she's wearing one of the nightgowns she had when I was little. I remember Mom telling me I shouldn't say anything about the sleeves, about how warm she must have been in the summertime, because she was self-conscious about her scar.

"Are you feeling better?" I ask when she opens the door.

The hall light's off, and she looks tired in the shadows, but she tells me she's fine and starts apologizing about missing Dad's thing.

"It's not a big deal," I say. "I barely got to talk to anyone, there were so many people."

She smiles, a little.

"Anyway, I found these in my closet."

She takes the polaroids from me and shuffles through them, and I wonder if I should have thrown them out. Her face doesn't really tell me anything, and she says the *that's so thoughtful*s and *how* *sweet of you*'s and *I'll enjoy these*'s that you can't tell are sincere. We have these phrases ingrained from growing up here. They come out whenever we need them.

"So Brent's staying in town tonight?" I ask.

Bev reaches down and fiddles with something stuck to the bottom of her slipper. "I think so," she says.

"I meant to ask him how the concert went."

"Concert?"

"Saturday, in the city. With the people from work."

"Right," she says, then, "with Kym?"

I nod. And I don't know where we are now, if Bev's a go-between or if I am, like I used to be for them—women always talk more easily with girls—or if this is just normal, what Brent and I are doing, taking a step back from a life we haven't really lived together since we were kids. Maybe nothing's wrong with this.

"I think Kym's intern organized it. Leah," I say, finally.

Bev looks over her shoulder. "I'd tell you to come in," she says, "but I think I'm still getting over this bug. I don't want to give it to you."

"No, it's fine," I tell her. "I just wanted to drop the photos by."

"I'm making some soup. Squash—not your favorite, I know, but good for you. I can bring some by tomorrow, if that sounds good?"

I don't know what to say right away.

"You know it's like the minestrone, always better after a night in the fridge," she says.

I thank her, and I'm home before the sun's down.

Later, I'm checking all the doors to make sure they're locked when I think about Cody again. Maybe that's what's bothering me, remembering Brent thinking something bad about him.

I text Bev to ask what she knows about him. Paige is like one of those little, enclosed glass ecosystem orbs you used to be able to get at the rock store at the mall; you can't live inside one and not know every other element there.

*He's working on Martha's place*, she texts me back right away. *He's been over there a lot.*

*You know him well?*

*Not really.*

Later, as I'm turning on *Golden Girls*, Bev texts again.

*Did you ever think you and Brent would end up together?*

I read this a couple times and wonder if she's had wine. Or a hot toddy, like she used to make when she was sick. It must be that; she almost never drinks wine.

I start to type that Brent and I have always been good friends, then erase. I guess that's it, why she seems weird with me after he's been out somewhere with other women.

*I don't know*, I tell her.

# 51



*Prom, fifteen years earlier*

By eleven, there were only a few kids out doing the sprinkler and the robot on the dance floor. Everyone else was sitting around the vinyl-covered tables sprinkled with gold confetti or else taking their last pictures by the entrance to the high school gym, posing with the cardboard boat the prom planning committee had made look like the Titanic.

The chaperones were split between cleaning up at the punch tables and huddled in doorways squinting into the strobe lights.

Kara Peterson and Brent Thomas were alone at their table, like they usually were, and thinking about heading home. It was almost time. She was laughing at his impression of Parker Lange, who was a couple tables over with the other cheerleaders.

They'd almost settled on leaving, hoping to beat the traffic through the little bottleneck on St. Charles, when the chatter at Parker's table died down.

Dalton Rolenfeld had just come in—no one ever asked where he'd been—and he tossed an arm around Parker while one of the other girls took their picture from across the table. He and Parker were prom king and queen, and they stood out in the crowd; he was wearing the only tux in the place that wasn't rented, and her dress had come from some fancy boutique in the city. When the music slowed down and the DJ announced the last song, they led a kind of informal procession back to the dance floor.

Kara and Brent decided to dance, too, at the last minute. They were trying to get away from the middle of the floor, from Parker and Dalton and all the others who rushed to fill in around them, and Kara almost stepped on Kym Hartmann's shoes over by the bleachers. Kym was sitting there alone, baby blue tulle spread out around her that was almost identical to Kara's pink. Maybe her dad was the same in thinking she should be a princess, too.

Some kids had already slipped out by the time the song was winding down, and Brent was getting Kara's shawl from their table when the DJ announced one last song, another slow one.

Kara was waiting in the doorway and didn't see Dalton come up behind her. She didn't see Parker Lange, either, glaring at her from across the gym before rushing into the girls' bathroom.

Dalton leaned in close to Kara's face, like the music was still loud, to ask her to dance.

Everyone saw, of course. Even with Parker fuming in the bathroom with a couple of her friends, they had an audience. Cody Muller almost let go of Stacey Becker, another of the cheerleaders, when Dalton led Kara out to the middle of the floor, and Alicia

Evans let out a little shriek and started taking pictures with her new digital camera.

Kara didn't see any of them. She couldn't stop looking at Dalton as he linked his arms behind her waist and pulled her in close, spinning her in slow circles under the disco ball.

A little ways into the song, Brent asked Kym Hartmann, but they danced with a few inches of space between their bodies and spent the whole time looking at Kara and Dalton. The tulle at the front of Kara's dress was smushed into Dalton's legs, and the two of them looked, everyone said afterwards, just like a couple.

# 52



*Sebastian*


Kara's on her Social app again. I can see everything she clicks on, every time she stops to read a post in her feed or scrolls on by.

The browser on the cloned phone has a VPN, though I doubt she'd notice if I started to mess with her, to make posts from her account or send emails or something. Kara's not suspicious like that.

She goes back to the search bar after a little scrolling and types *Cody Muller* next to the magnifying glass. She hovers over his picture for a couple seconds before she clicks on his profile. She'll go through his photos next, I think, or maybe look at some posts on his wall.

I want to mess with her now, but I click out, because I need this phone to last.

# 53

*Kara*

Brent comes over a couple hours after he gets off work Wednesday night. I don't know why I jump when he knocks, why I feel like I don't know what to expect when I get to the door. I keep it locked now, even during the day.

He looks normal, of course, like he always does. He has a big tupperware container of Bev's squash soup with him, and I try to act like I'm normal, too, as I put it in the fridge.

I don't know why it seems like it's been so long since we've talked. It hasn't. And we used to go so much longer. I babble for a while just to make noise, asking him about how Bev's feeling and how Kym's thing for HR's going and whether he wants something to eat—the soup, maybe, or we could order some pizza.

"I'm all right," he tells me. "We went out after work." He's facing away, on the sofa already. "But you should eat something. You've been getting skinny."

I tell him I've eaten, too, and almost ask who the *we* is, but this shouldn't bother me, Brent going out with people from work. Or with anyone else. When I think about it, it *doesn't* bother me. I guess it's just this bit of residual awkwardness, wondering for the first time if there's something we're not talking about.

We decide to watch a movie before we've really managed to get a conversation going, and he goes over to the cabinet under the TV. He picks another nineties romcom, one we watched at the Six sometime in middle school.

I watch this time as he presses the buttons. He's the only person who's ever gotten along with our DVD player. I thought Dad would have replaced it after we went away to college, but he never did.

The movie's one we can talk through, one we can be normal through, I think, like we used to be. It starts to feel better once it gets going, at least, with my feet up over Brent's knees and my back against the pillows at the side of the sofa like usual. They have a permanent dent I still fit inside. Dad must have never flipped them around.

Just when I'm thinking how normal things are, Brent shifts to face me.

"Have you been sleeping all right?" he asks.

I look away from the screen. I don't know why we haven't been laughing. This one's supposed to be funny.

"Fine," I tell him.

"You know I could stay here," he says, because of course he doesn't believe me.

I think about this, probably more than I should. "It's not that," I say.

"What is it, then?"

I don't know why I lie now. I'm not sure I even know what the truth is. "I think I'm just stressed," I say. "You know, about the house."

Brent looks around the living room then like he's just seeing it. All the piles have been moved out to the garage now. A good vacuuming will take care of what's left in the carpet.

"It looks better," he says. "You're making progress."

I nod and turn the TV volume up a notch, like maybe I'm just missing something in the dialogue, something that would make this movie as funny as it was the last time we watched it.

"You're really gonna put the house on the market?" Brent asks when I think we're done talking.

I look at the remote but don't press pause. "I don't know when." But that's not what he's asking, not really. The plan was always for me to leave again, to go back to the city. I don't know why that would change.

"You said work was going good from here. You wouldn't really have to go back to the office much, would you?"

I pause the movie but keep my eyes on the screen. "Maybe some in February and March."

"So you could stay."

I don't know how to respond to this. I *could* stay.

"You haven't gotten any more notes or anything?" he asks.

I shake my head and sit up, reaching for my coffee mug. Maybe that's it, why I can't sleep, all the coffee. Maybe this is a genetic thing. My dad and grandfather were big coffee drinkers, too. Sometimes things are part of us like this without our knowing why. Like whatever Brent and I are now, we grew into naturally, unavoidably.

"You didn't tell me about the concert," I say after a minute, to change the subject.

"It was good."

"Yeah?"

Brent takes his feet down from the ottoman. My feet are already on the floor.

"What is it?" he asks.

"Nothing." But he knows my 'nothing's as well as I know his.

It takes me a while to ask him about Leah. We used to talk so easily about these things, but this is different. I don't know what to ask, so I just ask if she liked the music.

"Yeah," he says. "I thought I told you she got the tickets."

"You did." I reach for the remote again.

He's faster, grabbing it off the ottoman. "Kara," he says.

"I'm sorry," I tell him. "It's just stress." I can feel him watching me as I stare at the paused movie. It's on one of those closeups of faces in the rain right before they kiss.

"Can we be honest about this?" he asks.

"Of course." Because we always have been before.

"Good. Because you know I'm here. And I'm gonna be here, anytime you want me to be."

I start to say something, but I'm not really sure what—it's gratitude, I think, or something else that's not quite right tonight.

"You understand?" he asks.

I nod. I don't know how long things have been this way and I didn't really know, or I didn't look at it closely, or I just wasn't ready. That's what I've been saying about dating for the last decade, that I wasn't ready.

Brent reads my mind. "It's been ten years, Kara."

And that's my cue to start with the excuses—for why I haven't dated and why I didn't finish law school, not for why Brent and I haven't gotten together, because I never thought of that as a real possibility before. But they all stick in my throat.

"Look, you know I'm not in a hurry." He laughs, then, so I laugh, too, but my laughs aren't right tonight, either.

"I'm not trying to rush you or anything," he says.

"I know," I say, when it seems like he expects me to say something.

He wraps an arm around my shoulder. It's easy to fall into him, then, gravitationally. My head goes to his chest like it used to whenever there was something wrong, something not like this.

I don't know how long we stay like this, with my spine bent and his arms around me, before I sit up. I know he's going to kiss me before he does. It's weird, I think, that we haven't done this before, in high school or sometime else. You'd think we would have at least tried it out at some point.

When you know someone as well as I know Brent, you assume you know how they kiss. I don't, though, until his lips tough mine. He tastes like the Dr. Pepper he used to drink. Maybe he hasn't cut back as much as he says he has.

After a few seconds, I pull away.

"You okay?" he asks.

I nod and sit back, and I can't tell him how much I wish this felt right.

# 54

*Sam*

Thursday night, I'm home from my shift and just scrolling my Social feed when there's a soft chime and a notification at the bottom of my screen. It's the private window for the camera at Kara's, letting me know it's detected something.

It's probably just a squirrel, I think as I wait for the video to load, or another raccoon.

When the little wheel stops spinning and it plays, it's nothing, at first, and then everything goes black, left to right.

It freezes me to my chair, tenses every muscle in my back. I can't even say for sure that it's a person. It's like something out of a horror movie when the thing passes right in front of the camera so you can't see its face.

I play it again and get the same feeling. Then I look at the time stamp—less than five minutes ago—and run for my car.

Kara's still up when I get to her house, just out of a shower and wrapped in a fuzzy blue robe.

I sit at the kitchen island and watch as she puts on an old tea kettle. She remembered I don't drink coffee.

"I was just close by," I tell her, trying to keep my voice casual, but my pulse hasn't settled yet. I guess some things still trigger this. "I was driving around this side of town."

Kara smiles. "Perfect timing," she says. She changes the grounds in the coffee machine and gets out a couple mugs as she waits for the kettle to boil.

I look past her, into the darkness outside the glow of the floodlights, and wonder if I could ever be as relaxed as she seems to be here. I've lived in cities all my life, where there's always some light and noise, and I think out here that I'd start to hear and see things even if they weren't real.

But there *was* someone real threatening her with the notes, and I really think it was someone I saw on the computer, too, even though it was just a flash of darkness. I wish I could tell her I saw something with the camera I set up on her property without her permission and get Baer to take it seriously, too. But he'd call this ghost hunting if I told him. Illegal ghost hunting. I went all the way around the house when I got here and didn't see anything, so I think he'd use the word 'obsessed,' and he'd probably point out that I'm a little haunted, too.

The coffee maker gurgles in the background as Kara pours out my tea. Then she sits down on the other barstool and starts to thank me, like she always does. She's calm tonight, I think, too calm for what's happening, and I wonder if she was always calm, reporting the rape and afterwards. Maybe she learned that from her dad, that women don't get taken seriously when they react like men would.

"So how much longer do you think you'll be in town?" I ask. My breathing's finally settled.

"I'm not really sure," Kara says.

"I was just looking at some security systems and thought of you. One of those might not be a bad idea for you to have here. They can help sell houses in rural areas like this."

"Really?"

I nod. "Nicer homes like this one, especially. More and more people are getting them. There are basic models with just a button to push in case you need anything—fire, ambulance, police..."

Kara looks towards the living room windows then, out through the trees that meet the Rolenfelds' land. "That's a good idea," she says.

I tell her I'll send her some links for good models that aren't too expensive, and we stay there in the kitchen talking for a while, about real estate in the area and clearing out cramped closets from our teenage years like I really am just here to chat.

When I leave, I take a few steps back into the woods and watch through the windows as Kara locks the door behind me and goes upstairs. I wait until she's out of sight to leave the little circle of light and check on the camera.

It's fine, still hidden in the branches. I look for footprints in the mud around it with the flashlight on my phone, but I can't see anything through all the leaves.

Cody looks surprised to see me at Martha's place just a few

minutes later.

"What is it?" he asks as soon as he opens the door. "Is Kara..."

"She's fine."

I follow him in through the entryway, where the kitchen used to be, and think of the bright blue tiles that were here on my first visit. There's a beautiful upgraded kitchen on the other side of the house now Cody finished before he started on the conservatory.

"Something's wrong," he says.

I take a seat on the leather sofa and look out through the windows. The outside lights aren't on, and I can't see past Martha's garden in the moonlight.

"I don't know," I admit.

"Did Kara get another note, or…"

"No. I was just over there talking to her. I think she's getting a security system."

"Good," Cody says, then, "I shoulda thought of that."

I reach into the pocket of my jacket, to the stun gun there.

"I'll check in with her tomorrow," he says. "When it comes, I can install it right away. They're quick."

I nod. "I think maybe it's good you're here. Next door, I mean."

He waits, like he does.

I don't know what to say that he won't see through. That's something I didn't expect when I first met Cody. I guess he pays more attention than most people do.

"I had this," I say, finally, and get out the stun gun. It looks just like a cell phone, but like one of those really old, block-style models like the one Martha uses with big buttons for her arthritis.

Cody reaches out a hand and takes it from me.

"I can't actually give it to her," I say.

He stares at it. It looks small in his hand.

"It's a stun gun," I offer.

"Okay," he says.

"Okay," I say, and sit back into the cushions.

# 55

*Kara*

I don't realize until Friday night that I'm almost out of milk. Gleson's isn't busy when I get in, so I pick up the rest of my list, too, another half dozen yogurts and a few each of some fruits and vegetables and the little frozen chocolate muffin top things that are supposed to be full of vitamins.

I'm almost to the checkout line when I see Kym Hartmann in the wine aisle.

We're too close to turn away, but I think she's going to until I say her name.

We do the usual Paige routine then, acting like we're friends even though we just went to high school together and have homes within a couple miles of each other now. Kym tells me what a nice job I did for my dad's celebration of life and asks how I'm handling the house, and I compliment her new haircut and ask about her little sister in Oregon.

There's a pause when we've run out of these things to say to each other.

"So how was the concert?" I ask.

"Concert?"

"Saturday." I try to remember the band. It started with an *M*, I think, and wasn't one I'd heard of before. I don't know most of them anymore, though.

Kym doesn't say anything.

"In the city," I prompt. "Brent said Leah got the tickets?"

Kym has that little half frown like she used to get around us in high school. I never knew what it was, exactly—disapproval, I think, but she never said anything to us. Maybe she hasn't changed much. Maybe she hasn't had to.

"I wasn't invited," she says after a couple seconds.

"Oh." I try to think of something else to say, but I don't come up with it. I must have wanted to think Saturday night was a work thing, not a date with Leah thing, but of course that's on me. Did Brent even say it was a work thing? I wouldn't have asked.

Kym's really frowning when I finally manage to say something about the cold front expected this weekend and hurry to the checkout lane.


I can't stop thinking about the concert when I get back to the house. I don't know why it bothers me so much; it's not like Brent lied to me, exactly. And it shouldn't matter to me either way, if he went on a date with Leah or not.

I'm still thinking about him and Leah even after I've showered, even after I've changed into my pajamas and turned on the house channel for some noise. I pick up my phone a couple times, writing texts I don't send—basic ones asking how he's doing. *What* he's doing. If work was okay. If he's ready for the weekend, whatever that means. None of them sound right.

I think the next move's mine, since he made the first one—or the biggest one, at least, when he kissed me. He's just giving me space now to figure out what I want to do, after all the times I've said I'm not ready.

I finally call him a little before eight, tired of picking up my phone and setting it back down again.

"Sorry," I say as soon as he answers. "Are you busy?"

"'s okay," he says. "You okay?"

"Fine," I tell him, and then the line's quiet for a second.

"You're in town? At your place?" I ask.

"Are you okay?" he repeats.

"Yeah. Fine." But my voice doesn't sound right. I think Brent doesn't sound like he usually does, either, that this is uncomfortable for both of us. But maybe that's in my head, too.

"Good," he says.

"I saw Kym Hartmann."

"What?"

It's not what I meant to say, how I meant to start this.

There's a pause. "And?"

"The thing Saturday," I say. "The concert. She told me she didn't go."

"She didn't."

"Was it like...a date, then? You and Leah?"

I can hear his exhale this time, slow. "Yeah," he says, finally, "I guess something like that. I didn't really know what to call it when I told you about it. Are you upset?"

"No." Of course I'm not upset. I don't have any reason to be upset. It's just that he's never hidden anything from me before. "No," I say again.

"You sure?"

"I just thought it was a work thing."

"Let's talk about this," Brent says, like we used to be able to. "You know I..."

"No, really," I tell him, "it's fine."

"Kara."

"It wasn't any of my business. I'm sorry."

His breath's loud. Or maybe it's mine. "I don't want you to be sorry," he says. "Anyway, it was casual, not a big deal. You know this isn't the same. She's not you."

"I'm sorry," I repeat, and I'm not really sure what I'm sorry for this time.

We keep repeating ourselves until we wear this out, but I don't feel any better at the end of the call than I did at the beginning.

I don't know how long I've been sitting on the sofa after I hang up with Brent that my phone buzzes again.  I pull my feet off the other cushion—I don't fit right here without Brent's legs—and open the message.

It's Cody. *Too late to come by?* he asks. *Got the new lock for the balcony.*

*Great,* I tell him. *Thanks.*

I go to my old bathroom to put up my hair and dot my cheeks with some blush, but I still don't look right when I study my reflection in the mirror.

"You okay?" Cody asks when I open the front door a few minutes later.

"Fine," I tell him, and make myself smile. I have to remember he can't see something's wrong just from looking at me, like Brent can.

"Sorry," he says, "I meant to get back here earlier. Been up at a supplier in Dale."

"It's okay. I'll be up for a while." Longer than a while, probably. The microwave clock says it's only 8:31.

"You a night owl?" he asks.

"Kind of." I seem to be one in Paige, anyway.

"Okay day?" he asks as I follow him through the living room, because maybe it's obvious something's wrong with me.

"Maybe a little stressful. It's work," I tell him, because I'm not sure what else to say it is.

I follow Cody through my old bedroom, where he goes right to the door to the balcony. "So there's something with the lock?" I ask.

He grabs the handle and jiggles it. The bar slides around and then shifts to the side, unlocking the door.

"You didn't know?"

"I don't...I guess I don't go out there anymore."

Cody looks at me, then at the window. If he were just a couple steps outside, he could see the light at the end of the Rolenfeld's dock.

"Easy fix," he tells me.

I watch him work for a few minutes as he kneels on the carpet and unscrews the old lock. I don't expect it to, but a whole chunk of the door just pulls out then, leaving a hole cool air comes rushing in through.

"You learned this from your dad?" I ask, pulling my wrap tighter around my shoulders.

"Some of it. I did a lot with Schaffer's, though, too. Summers in high school and for a few years after."

"Right," I say, like I followed this, like I really knew him before. "Was it tough, working with your dad before that?"

He keeps his eyes on a screw. "My parents are all right," he says. "They were supportive and all. I was just ready to go off on my own."

"Sure." I watch his hands work for a while, aligning the screws with the handle and then taking the whole thing back out again. I'm struck by how different Cody is than Brent, or at least by how different this feels. Maybe they're not actually different at all; maybe it's just that I don't know Cody well. And I'm not really used to being around other men.

"I saw them at the gala," I say. "Your parents. They looked good."

"Yeah. They're doin' good."

I'm trying to think of other things to ask him about when he sits back and looks at me again.

"Sam said you were lookin' at security systems," he says.

"Uh huh. Do you normally put them in? In renovations or anything, I mean?"

He nods. "They're good." Then he bends to line up the new door handle in the empty space. "If nothin' else, they make people feel more secure."

"Right," I say, because I guess I'm one of those people now, someone who needs to feel more secure.

I watch as Cody uses the electric drill to screw in the new lock, then does the same for the door handle. When he tries it afterwards and flips the bolt, nothing jiggles.

"That's better," I say. "Thanks so much for this. I need to write you a check."

He stands up. "I had one of these locks around. It's no problem."

"Let me at least get you some coffee, then."

"You've got coffee on? This late?"

"I was going to," I lie. "It's not that late."

He smiles. "You're a lot like your dad. He was out at The Strawberry at all kindsa hours."

I want to say something witty, to find some other thing my dad and I had in common, but sometimes I'm not sure that we really were anything alike. "You, too?" I ask. "You're a big coffee drinker?"

"I guess." Cody's voice is softer behind me as he follows me to the kitchen. He goes to the other side of the island again when I put on the coffee pot, but he doesn't sit down.

I ask him how Martha's conservatory's going as the machine starts to burble behind me. This isn't like talking to most other people in Paige, who make the conversation for you; Cody doesn't go on about the weather or pretend we knew each other back in the day, reminiscing.

"Talked to Martha today," he says. "She's sorry to miss you, says she hopes you'll stay on through Christmas."

"I'm sorry to miss her, too." I don't know what to say about staying until Christmas. I *could* stay until Christmas, I know. It wouldn't affect my work at all.

I pour out the coffees and give him his mug. "I was just trying to remember from high school. You have a brother, don't you?"

He waits to pick up his coffee until I've stepped back to my side of the island. "Brad," he says.

"That's it. I thought he was a couple years ahead of me. He played football, too, didn't he?" That's what I remember about Cody, seeing him in his football jersey around the hallways.

Cody nods. "He still keeps up with it, plays in a friendly league up in Cleveland."

I take a tiny sip of my coffee. It burns my lips. We're quiet for a minute. But this is an okay quiet, I think.

I want to ask him about Dalton. Because he knows him better, or at least he must have back in high school, since they were on the football team together. Maybe he'd know who Dalton's real friends were, if there's anyone with a name like Sebastian. I open my mouth, but I don't know how to ask any of this.

"I hope you feel safe here," Cody says then. "Like you don't have to go back to the city unless you want to."

"Thanks. I've been thinking about it, actually."

"Staying?"

"Not long term." I swallow a sip of coffee, burning my throat.

"Or I guess I'm not really sure."

"The house bring back memories?"

"Not here," I say automatically, even though I don't have a good reason not to keep the house if I do stay. "I'll put it on the market when it's ready."

Cody sets his mug back on the counter. "Almost forgot," he says. "I meant to give you this when I got here." He reaches into a pocket and pulls out an old school-style cell phone.

I stare at it for a second, at the buttons that aren't quite right.

"It's a stun gun," he says.

I come around the island next to him and pick it up. It has numbers like a phone, but there's a big button in the middle that says "stun" in red letters.

I look back at Cody. I don't know how to ask him why he has it. Or why he's giving it to me.

He points to a slider on the top. "You move this," he says. The whole thing lights up red when he does. "Then you press that button. The electricity comes out here..."

I watch his hands as he explains how it works.

"You think I need a stun gun," I say at the end.

He shifts his weight away from me. "A friend gave it to me. That's all. I don't need it."

I look up at him. I can't imagine why anyone would give Cody Muller a stun gun.

"Just figure it's better to have it," he says, "and not need it."

I thank him and pick it up, pushing the slider back to turn off the light.

He gets a folded sheet of paper out of his pocket. Men always have pockets like this, nothing like ours that can't hold anything, that can't hide anything. The paper's directions, just a few sentences in bold print.

"So you turn it on," he says, taking another step away from me as he points to the side of the phone. "And you wait until...It doesn't shoot or anything like that. You hold it and act like you're dialin' the phone until...until they reach for it, and then you press the button."

I look from his hand to the paper. It warns me not to put my fingers on the top, where the electricity comes out, or to leave it on in a pocket, where I could stun myself accidentally. And not to use it for more than a few seconds, or it can cause a heart attack. Or death.

It's simple otherwise. *Push the slider. Press "stun." Hold for no more than three seconds.*

"And that's it," Cody says, stepping back and putting the island between us again.

I thank him, and we sip our coffees quietly while I try to think of what to ask him next, anything but why I might need a stun gun.

# 56


*Sebastian's mom*

Saturday morning, I'm running late for book club. We've been having every third meeting on a Saturday recently instead of on the weekdays like they all used to be, when our husbands were at work and our kids at school. To be more inclusive, we said. Because we like to say that we're inclusive, that we welcome working women.

It's almost ten when I get to St. Luke's basement. It's crowded, but my usual seat in front of the coffee table's open. We stopped eating donuts and pretending we weren't all watching our weight a few years ago, so now we just have coffee and some mini muffins Lauren Merkel brings over from the bakery.

I've barely finished the book for this month, so maybe that's why I feel rushed when we start with Becky Lange's discussion questions a couple minutes past the hour. She's the leader this month since the book was her pick.

The twist comes up first, of course, like it always does. There's a twist at the end of all Becky's picks.

"I saw it coming," Parker, her daughter, says, because we like to think we can see these things coming. The twist was about the main character, the one you trusted all the way through. He wasn't the murderer, but he knew who was and looked the other way, making his wife think she was crazy.

"It's called gaslighting," Alicia Schmid says. She's young enough to know all the words they have for these things now.

"It's called *having a husband*," Lauren adds, and the others laugh.

It's my turn to say something. Sometimes it can take me too long with books like this. Probably I could say more about it than any of them, but maybe not; you can't always tell what someone's been through.

"What about her not being able to go out?" I ask, about the gaslit wife. Because I really could see the end right at the beginning of the book. "Or how he didn't want her talking to some of her friends?"

There's a pause. Maybe I'm the only one who noticed. I shouldn't be; from the beginning, this group has been a way for us to get away from our husbands. Because this isn't something they'd enjoy, we said. Most of us don't, either.

"Maybe he's a *little* controlling," Parker concedes after a minute. "But can you blame him?" This is part of a larger pattern, of course, how even a group of well-off, educated women can miss something so big. About him being just a *little* controlling, about there being *reasons*.

"Everybody has some bad days," Becky adds, something she would say. "And he never hit her or anything."

I don't respond, and some of the others chime in. The real

twist wasn't about the husband, I think, or even about his wife. To me, the twist was that they had a son, that this story isn't over.

"What about the son?" I ask. "Elliott."

Parker's brow wrinkles the way it used to at the top of the cheerleader pyramid on Friday nights, when you could barely see she was shaking. "What about him?" she asks.

I look down at my hands. They're shaking, too. "Don't you think this will affect him? What his father did?" I try to swallow, but my throat's dry. I should have gotten coffee. "Don't you think there's some risk he'll..."

I don't finish this, and I don't hear what the others say right away, what excuses they make, what excuses we always make for men like him.

I tune back in when Lauren's talking about what a good *provider* he is, whatever his flaws. Then I say I'm not feeling well and rush out, running all the way to my car.

# 57



*Sam*

I'm just back from my shift Saturday afternoon—another one I added— when Lisa calls.

"You're in the lab today?" I ask. She doesn't usually work on Saturdays.

"Just odds and ends," she tells me. "It was no problem to check out that stuff you sent. French vanilla powder, huh? Weird murder cases you get up there in the country."

I laugh, a little. "So could it have been that?"

"I guess theoretically, but it would have had to be a ton."

"How much?"

"Like most of the tub. There's only 50 milligrams a scoop."

I want to say I'm surprised the county coroner didn't flag this as suspicious, the sheriff turning up with an early heart attack so full of caffeine. But I'm not, really.

"It was a lot in his blood," Lisa says. "And that powder has a bunch of other stuff in it too, like B vitamins. So you'd think those would be in the report if he'd taken that much."

I'm already online looking up Stubsen's powder. I can't find an unflavored version. And Stan would have tasted a fist full of french vanilla powder in his coffee, or the chocolate flavor.

"So it's probably not the powder," I say. I can't tell her why I want it to be so badly. Not because I want to be sure it's Stubsen, but because I want to think that whoever it is, I can know. You always want to think you can tell, that you can catch people like this.

"Anyway, I'd bet on caffeine pills," Lisa says. "The capsules would have dissolved by the time they did the autopsy. Or somebody could have emptied them into his drink."

I sit back in my desk chair and click on the browser window with Kara's camera. It hasn't picked up anything for a while.

"A caffeine pill?" I ask.

"You can get them anywhere. Online or wherever."

I turn on the camera's live feed. When it loads, I squint into the shadows like maybe I'll see something new there tonight.

"You're okay?" Lisa asks.

"Sorry, yeah. Thanks a lot."

There's a second I think the phone's cut out. "So you think the death is connected to the rape kit?" she asks. "This probably isn't a great case for you."

"Probably not," I agree. When she's waiting for me to say something else, I click out of the browser, and my normal screen loads. "Do you think you could run some DNA against the kit?"

"You can get DNA?"

I take a breath to think this through. But I made the decision a while ago, really. "Just two guys," I tell her.

"You can get it?" Lisa repeats.

"Unofficially."

I think for a second she's going to ask what good it does to know when you can't use the results to prosecute. But she just says she'll run whatever I can get.

# 58



*Kara*

Saturday night, I lock myself in the upstairs bedroom—I don't think of it as my dad's room anymore, now all his things are gone. Now it's just where I go to get away from the ground floor windows, where I sit up each night and go through the foods I've eaten and the steps I've taken and everything else I've done through the day and pretend that remembering all of this is enough to let me sleep.

Tonight, I'm listening to the drone of the TV like usual. I have it on one of those sitcoms with a constant laugh track.

I told Brent I was working late, getting things in order. I guess that could mean for staying in Paige or for leaving.

After I've paid my rent in Shaker Heights, there's nothing else productive for me to do. I'm all caught up on a couple client reports, and things won't pick up at the office until December for year-end giving. There's still no reason for me to go back.

So there's just a text document up on my screen as I click into the TV guide and select *Saturday Night Live*.

I watch the opening monologue and try to laugh in the right

places, to get back to nights like this by myself being normal like they would be in the city, to *feeling* normal again.

I look back at the text document when it goes to commercial.

*Sebastian*

*Crickets*

*Wrong time on the clock—no train*

These are the things I still don't understand from that night. Because I guess it's not enough that I know *who*, or at least one who, or that I know why Dalton didn't have to drag me up the stairs. It's not even enough that I know I was responsible, in that moment, for what was about to happen.

Maybe that's what I can't shake, the guilt. Both of my therapists said that, told me over and over how common misplaced guilt is. It comes from the questions we're asked about what we were wearing and what we were doing and the narrative we use when we talk about it, how women *are raped* like we go to the grocery store and do all the other things we do, not how a man *rapes* a woman, the perpetrator with the action verb.

The other text column has the times I don't remember—the shots, the pool table, and walking home, and then the things more recently, turning on the lights that first night with the scratching and the lotion I don't remember finding. And the crickets.

I don't have anything obvious to add to this list tonight, at least, no foods gone missing or extra steps on my watch, so after a few minutes, I close the laptop. I want to think that if I keep looking at the same things over and over, one day, they'll make sense. I'll see something I didn't before, and then everything else—

every little doubt, every irregularity, every wrong feeling I've ever had—will have a reason.

I turn up the volume after the commercial break and try to focus on the *SNL* skit. It's about the president, one of the funny ones. And it works, for a while. But that's the thing about these times that get lost; they don't happen when you think they should.

I'm watching the beginning of one of the regular segments when I hear the crickets. I look at the remote, but I can't make myself press the mute button.

It doesn't matter. The crickets just keep getting louder, even with the volume high. So loud I can't hear the laughter anymore.

They give me that robotic feeling again, like my arms and legs won't move when I tell them to. I don't know where I'd go, anyway, with the crickets in my head. They're still loud when I wrap my fingers around the phone on my nightstand.

I take a breath and count backwards then, like that first therapist taught me, thinking I was likely to have panic attacks even if they didn't start right away. It seems so strange now that I didn't.

I count the things I can see—the TV, the duvet, the windows, the door, and my phone. It's not like I can't breathe or like I'm going to have a heart attack, like everyone says about panic attacks. I look at my hands as I open my texts. They're not shaking, at least.

*Do you hear crickets?* I ask Cody. Then I let the phone fall to my side and sit back against the headboard.

I breathe for a while, like maybe I can breathe this away, and count.

I count heartbeats, the pounding in my head, until there's

pounding downstairs.

Later—I don't know how much later, but I can't hear my heart anymore—Sam's sitting on the barstool next to mine, and Cody's standing on the other side of the granite island again.

"There wasn't any scratching this time?" Sam asks me.

I shake my head.

"And all you heard were the crickets."

"Right."

"Only on that side of the house?" She looks up to Dad's bedroom.

"I think so." The crickets were quiet, of course, by the time I ran downstairs. Not just less noticeable, completely gone.

"You didn't hear them anywhere else?" Sam asks.

I shake my head. It was just my heartbeat once I got downstairs. I remember thinking it was part of the knocking at the door. "It was a panic attack," I tell her, because of course this is what happens during a panic attack, hearing your heartbeat. Panicking.

"No," Cody says. "You weren't panicking."

But I was. I had to be. I know crickets don't just turn on, loud, and then turn back off again. That's not how finding a mate works. It's a constant thing. "I could hear my heartbeat," I say. "That's a panic thing. I'm really..."

"What about a report?" Cody asks Sam.

"A police report?" I ask, and then apologize again. I shouldn't have texted him, shouldn't have made this sound like an emergency, this slow loss of what's real to me. I almost wish it *were* real, that there were some actual threat here. It would be easier if it were a person in my house, someone I could see, something I could understand, instead of just something I hear sometimes.

"I'm not sure we should report it," Sam says after a second of quiet.

So she thinks it was panic, too. Maybe she can tell by looking at me. She probably has a lot of experience with this.

"That's not it," she says. "I just don't want them to be able to point to anything that could discredit you down the line, and without any of the doors…"

"I understand," I say, and she tells me again that she believes me.

I look at Cody. I almost ran into him when I opened the door, almost ran straight out into the darkness. It was like I was running away from something when I came downstairs, not towards something.

"Her phone went dead," he says after a second. "I got the text and tried calling. It went right to voicemail."

Sam asks if she can see my phone, and I tell her it's on the bed upstairs. Cody stays, his arms braced on the island, when she goes to get it.

"Did you have the stun gun?" he asks.

"On the nightstand." I don't know why I didn't reach for it, panicking. "I'll bring it next time," I say.

We listen to Sam's steps on the staircase. A minute later, she comes back to the kitchen and plugs my phone into the outlet by the coffee machine.

"No texts," she says when it finally wakes up. The little *whoosh* is loud, or maybe it's just that quiet in here now. "And no more notes or anything?"

"No."

"Have you given any thought to a security system?"

"I ordered one online, a system."

"When does it get here?" Cody asks.

"Monday. Schaffer's said they could set it up sometime next week."

"I can do it," he says, "as soon as it comes."

I start to say that he doesn't have to do this, like he hasn't had to do any of this, but he shakes his head.

"I have time," he tells me. "It's no problem."

Sam sets my phone back on the counter, and then it's quiet again.

"I can stay," Cody says, but to Sam as much as to me. "I can stay over in the workshop if that's better. At night, just so somebody else is here."

I twist to look at him. He's still looking at Sam.

I want to say this isn't necessary, either, that what happened tonight was just panic. "I'm not using that bed," I say, instead. "My old one, on the main floor."

Cody nods.

And that's it. Sam says some things I can't really focus on right now, about increasing patrols on this side of town and wanting me to check in with her periodically, but eventually, she goes, leaving me and Cody in the kitchen.

He locks the door behind her, jiggling the deadbolt to test it like the one on the door to the deck. It doesn't give.

I thank him and apologize again.

He looks at me for a second like he's going to ask me something, but he doesn't. "I'll do the dishes," he says, "so you can go rest."

"I'm not going to sleep. I don't know why my phone died." I'm not sure why this matters to me now, like it might be worse to lose control of your devices when you've already lost control of your senses and your memories.

He doesn't respond right away.

"I charge it while I'm in the shower," I explain, even though I know there's no reason to tell him this, that it only makes me sound crazier. "The battery never runs out. I don't use it very often."

He looks over at the phone but doesn't reach for it.

"I'm not crazy," I tell him. I don't know why I need to say it out loud right now. "Or I wasn't, before. I know there aren't still crickets out. I don't hear any now. This isn't how I am."

"I know," he says, finally looking at me. "I believe you."

# 59



*Sam*

Sunday morning, I get to The Strawberry early and take the red leather booth that backs up to Dalton's. He's holding court today, giving handshakes to the throng from St. Luke's. It's a kind of farewell parade I assume will take up his Sundays until he moves to Washington at the end of the year.

I listen to a few of these exchanges—the high school principal, Mrs. Merkel from the bakery, the owner of one of the Mexican franchises across the street—as I push some eggs around on my plate. Dalton says the same things to all of them. It's rehearsed, repeated with the same inflection each time, about his hopes for a new era in Washington and what progress he'll bring home to Paige.

I look at my phone under the table while he's busy with one of the families from Felden whose name I should recognize. There are so many of these names that all sound alike, though, with extra *d*'s and *t*'s that make you feel like you're hacking up something when you say them.

I have an unread text from Cody. *Already there?* he asks.

*Had something to do*, I tell him. *I'll pick up something for you and Kara?*

*I can meet you*, he says. *Give me a few?*

*Maybe better if I meet you at Kara's*, I tell him. Because I don't want Cody to see what I'm about to do, and I need some time to figure out what to say to Kara when I see her. We get all this training about how to calm down civilians, how to talk to get them to trust you, to make them feel comfortable. There are never any seminars about how to tell someone they *should* be afraid.

*Did she sleep okay?* I ask.

*Fine*, Cody says.

She must be one of those people who's used to being afraid, I guess, who's really adapted.

*That's good.* I leave out my phone and wait for Cody to say something else, but he's not one to send a thumbs up or anything once we're finished talking.

So I wait. All I have to do is sit here long enough. Dalton takes his time eating, but he stops by my table when there's a little break in the traffic before St. Mark's lets out.

"Samantha Ellis," he says, squaring up to my booth.

I feign surprise. I walked in from the side door so I didn't have to look at him. I know him, I think, or at least I know how to get his attention. Men like Dalton are all the same this way.

He flashes a big smile—fake, but maybe he doesn't have a real one—and sits down across from me without waiting to be invited.

I take a sip of my tea. "Dalton," I say. "Actually, I've been meaning to get in touch with you."

He leans in, and I get a whiff of his aftershave. "Here on

official business?" he asks.

"Unofficial." I look at his forehead for a second, then at his teeth. I could count them, big, bright veneers that look like they glow in the dark.

It makes him uncomfortable, not having me talking yet, fawning over him. His jaw's clenched, waiting.

"I've been thinking about your place," I say after a few seconds, and raise my hand for the check as the waitress passes by. She's looking at Dalton enough for both of us.

"My place?" His smile's back, and I meet his eyes this time. I wonder what he looks like without these faces. There's probably a way to find out, to put him in a situation he doesn't have a line for, a face for. But that's not what I need this morning.

"I was wondering if your family has enough security. With you heading off to..."

I'm cut off when the waitress comes by.

"So you've been worried about me," Dalton says, turning his smile to the waitress. "Mind if I have a coffee?"

I smile back this time. "Not at all," I say.

I let Dalton charm me like he wants to, like he has to. He pays for my eggs, of course, and for Kara and Cody's to-go meals, and he leaves first. This is a power play, having somewhere to be, leaving someone off balance.

I'm so off balance that I knock over his empty coffee mug as I'm getting up. I bend down to get it and drop it into my purse, into a bag that's waiting there. Then I close the zipper and pick up the mints on the receipt tray before I leave.

*     *

Monday night towards the end of my shift, Stubsen tells me I'm looking tired. I yawn a few times and lean back in my chair to stretch.

"I didn't sleep well," I tell him. "Think I might need one of your coffees to make it through the night."

He slides off the corner of my desk. "Really?" he asks. "You wanna try one?"

"Make me a good one," I say.

He makes one for both of us, and we catch up for a while.

*     *

Tuesday, when Stubsen can't find his usual mug, I tell him I thought I put it back in the cabinet after we had our coffee. But you know me, scatterbrained.

"Not a big deal," he says. "Probably one of the other guys took it by accident."

"Maybe I didn't put it back in the right spot. I'm sorry."

He comes back to my desk holding a new mug, one of the plain blue ones this time.

"So let me guess," he says. "You've already got plans this weekend?"

"It's my friend's birthday."

His eyebrows go up. "Friend? Cody Muller?"

"*Friend,*" I say. "Lisa. My friend in Cincinnati."

"Oh yeah."

I point to the over-taped package at my feet. "Actually, this is part of her gift."

Stubsen looks at the package, then nods. "You know you're gonna have to go out with me one of these weekends," he says. "You can't be out of town all the time."

I smile and tell him I'll take his word for it.

# 60



Tuesday evening, Cody gets back to the house just as dusk is settling over the trees. He stopped at Gleson's tonight on his way home from Dale and is making us tacos.

I watch him from across the island. This is the standard unit of distance he keeps between us now, one granite island. I thought having him here would be awkward since I've lived alone for so long, but I really only see him in the evenings, and he's quiet, unobtrusive. He leaves before I get out of bed in the mornings, and I listen to him close the door and lock it with an extra key I found in one of the kitchen drawers before I fall back asleep. I've wondered some at the irony of sleeping through these last few nights, at it being a man in the house that makes me feel safe here again.

"So anyone sick on your crew?" I ask, because I still don't really know what to talk to him about, what people talk about in situations like these, or probably not like these.

Some ground beef from one of the local farms—Schneider's, I think—simmers on the stove. He's been stirring it around.

"Because of flu season picking up," I say. "I saw on the news there were a lot of cases already this year."

Cody glances back at me as he washes off the spatula. "Yeah?" he asks. "Nobody yet."

"That's good. Bev's sick. Or she was, but she didn't think it was the flu."

"Maybe it's the weather," he says. "It's been gettin' cold pretty quick."

"Maybe." I can see the little lines of fog on the windows today, and the temperature's supposed to drop more this weekend. They say we might even get a dusting of snow, one of those early ones that barely covers the leaves and makes a bumpy, speckled carpet across the woods.

"So are you catching up with Sam soon?" I ask.

"We usually get together Sundays. We get breakfast at The Strawberry. You should come."

I shake my head, but he can't see me, focused on the meat again. "I wouldn't want to butt in," I say.

"You wouldn't be."

"How long have you been..." I don't know what word to use here. I guess I don't know a lot of words I should, by this age.

"Been friends since she came to town," he offers after a second. "It was a little while after your dad passed away."

"That's good she had you to show her around." I watch for a minute as he stirs the meat. "I'm grateful," I say. "To both of you."

He turns and pushes a bowl of salsa across the island. "Try this," he says.

I wait until he's facing the stove again, then dip in a chip and taste it.

"My mom's recipe. She sent it over."

"She knows you're here?"

He shakes his head. "Didn't want her to worry," he says.

I wonder whether Cody's mom *should* worry about him being here with me. I would, I think, if someone told me my story.

"How's Brent?" he asks as he's getting out the taco shells.

A chip sticks my throat, and I cough. "He's coming over tomorrow night. They're off at the factory Thursday for Rolenfeld's birthday." It's a tradition, apparently, that started when Bob Rolenfeld was actually working there, before he went to Washington.

"Right," Cody says.

I don't know what else to tell him about Brent, or about me and Brent. I still feel like I don't know what we are right now, or what I want us to be.

Cody sets the cheese out on the counter. "Why don't you let me know when he leaves," he says. "I'll stay over at Martha's until I hear from you."

"It's not…" I stop. I don't know what I'm saying, or what I should be. "Okay," I manage after a second. "I haven't told him you're here, like you asked, but you can be here whenever. It wouldn't be weird, I mean. Brent and I, we're friends."

Cody's quiet as he finishes stuffing my taco and pushes the plate across the island.

*     *

Wednesday night, Brent comes by a couple hours after he's done with work. He's already taken a shower and put on some sweats. He's eaten, too, he says, but he goes to the fridge to get a beer. My dad left a bunch of six-packs in the pantry, and I've been cooling them for when Brent comes over, and now for Cody, too. I don't think Cody's taken any, though.

Brent pauses in front of the refrigerator. "You're cooking now?" he asks.

I turn and see the leftover taco meat cocooned in saran wrap through the open door. "Just tacos," I say.

"Didn't have you pegged for it."

I open my mouth and almost tell him I wasn't the one who made the tacos—that maybe there are things I keep from him, too—but I change the subject, instead. "Work going okay?"

"Fine." He takes a beer bottle and pops off the top with his keychain. "I've been wanting to talk to you about it, actually."

I think of Leah first and catch myself this time, trying to gauge how I feel. Sometimes you have to sneak up on feelings like these. But I don't feel anything when I think about Brent and Leah. So maybe I'm not jealous, exactly.

"Not about that," he says, reading my mind the way he does. "Leah's not important to me. I told you that already."

I don't say anything as I follow him to the sofa. He picks my feet up, sets them over his knees like this night could be any other.

"I was just thinking it's kinda shitty, you know, me working for Dalton's company after everything you've gone through."

I tell him it's fine. I actually forget sometimes Brent works there. I don't really associate the place with Dalton, either, and of course almost everyone in Paige works for the Rolenfelds, one way or another.

"You don't feel safe here," Brent says, twisting to look at me. "I know you don't. I can see it. And I hadn't really thought about that before."

I want to tell him I *do* feel safe here, at least most of the time. I've felt safe for the last few nights, anyway, with the security system installed and with Cody downstairs.

"I'm not sure I feel *un*safe," I say when Brent seems to be waiting for me to say something. "Anyway, I think it's getting better. Maybe it was just the adjustment, like you said, coming home after all this time."

"But if you don't, we don't have to stay here."

*We.* He's looking ahead now, at the TV screen that's still black, not at me.

"We could go somewhere, is what I'm saying."

"Where?"

"Does it matter?"

We sit with the quiet between us for a little while.

"It's just something to think about," he says. "It's been on my mind lately, and you'll have a house to trade soon. We could go wherever you wanted."

I nod and try to keep my face quiet. Maybe the *we*'s are actually what's normal about this. It's always been *we*, through all the normal childhood stuff and the bigger bump afterwards I had no idea was part of a mountain I'd get lost on. I don't know what I thought would happen without a *we*, what constant there could possibly be in my life but Brent. This relationship's the only one I really know how to do, the only one I could expect to go well.

I don't say anything when he gets up to get a movie like he has probably hundreds of times before either of us had to think about what these nights might mean. He picks Disney this time, the boxed set he used to bring to Columbus with him. That was when my therapist first told me not to watch scary movies, afraid they'd feed my nightmares.

"What about *Beauty and the Beast*?" he asks.

I agree, and he fiddles with the DVD player the way only he knows how to. When he sits back down, he pulls my legs up over his knees. Our bodies fall away from each other as we watch the movie, and it's almost comfortable, I think, like it used to be.

"I shouldn't have gone to that concert with Leah," Brent says in a slower part between some songs. He's looking at me now.

"Of course you should have."

"No," he says. "I told you before, but you should know. I was just frustrated, not thinking right. It won't happen again."

I don't know what to say, so we go back to looking at the screen.

I get lost in how usual this is, how normal, and I don't think of Cody and this secret I'm keeping from Brent until we've paused the movie midway through and I'm scooping up some caramel fudge ice cream at the island. Brent's disappeared into my old bedroom to use that bathroom, and I don't think about Cody's things until he's already in there.

I stub my toe on my dad's armchair rushing to the door. But when I get to the doorway, my bedroom looks the same as always. The comforter's pulled up over the pillows how I've always made it, and Cody must have hidden his things underneath. I hear water running in the bathroom and the squeak of the towel bar as Brent dries his hands.

"You okay?" he asks when he slides open the pocket door.

"Yeah." I try to shake this funny little panic, to calm my heartbeat I can hear again. "Just waiting to go."

"I'll get the ice cream," Brent says. He touches my arm as he passes me, and I wonder if this will ever feel normal again.

Once he's gone, I close the bathroom door behind me and get out my phone to text Cody.

*Brent's staying*, I tell him. He brought a toothbrush with him tonight, laid out his dop kit on the table when he came in, I guess so this wouldn't come up.

I watch the phone for a minute as I'm washing my hands. I want to add a *thanks*, or even an *I'm sorry*, but I'm not sure which, so I don't say either.

A few seconds later, the little "read" check mark appears, and Cody writes, *I'll be next door. Let me know if you need anything.*

When I come out, Brent's leaning against the kitchen island and frowning at his phone.

"Everything okay?" I ask.

He rolls his eyes. "Work," he says.

"Do you need to call someone? It's okay."

"They can wait," he tells me. He hands me my ice cream then, and we go back to the sofa like usual.

# 61



*Sebastian's mom*

He shouldn't be back soon, but that doesn't stop me from checking the front drive again. There's always a little sparkle I imagine from the road that could be headlights. I used to miss them sometimes with his dad.

Tonight, I make myself go up the stairs. It's not like I haven't been in his room before; I used to come up here all the time when he was younger.

My feet sink into the carpet on the stairs, and it's like my whole body's sinking, slowing down. I shouldn't have to stop on the landing to catch my breath.

I'll say I was looking for something, I tell myself, if he comes back and finds me. Maybe I'm just after some baby things deep in his closet that I'm wanting to donate.

I pause at his door. I can't stop thinking about what I still don't know, what I haven't been sure about for so long now. I don't even know what to look for, really, if this kind of thing leaves traces. And what will I do if there *is* something? My mind keeps going to Kara, but of course I can't tell her. Maybe I'd send a note, anonymous, to that new female cop. Because what else could I do, other than see this coming? A mother's supposed to know her son better than anyone does.

I tell myself as I open the door that his behavior hasn't changed. So maybe I really am just looking for things to donate.

His room's tidy, like it's always been, from the time he was little. His bed's made. That came from his dad, making things look right when they weren't.

I glance at the window. This one faces the road. It's dark. No cars drive by this way at night.

I go to the laptop sitting on his desk. I don't even know what I'm wanting to rule out by doing this; probably not seeing anything that jumps out at me here still wouldn't be enough to stop the paranoia. I'm sure my son knows how to hide things as well as I do.

The laptop lights up as soon as I lift the screen. He must have left it on.

And then I don't have to wonder anymore. An internet window's open. There are a bunch of tabs, but the first one, his email, stops me.

It's that his email isn't his email, isn't his name. It's *Sebastian182*, nothing like the name I gave him when I thought he would be different, when I thought, at least, that he couldn't be his father.

There's a chat screen I can't look at for very long in the next tab with women he's said things to, things I'm not even sure he got from his dad. There are so many of them—girls, really, not women.

I read through a couple of these threads before clicking the next tab, an online game of some kind with a fairy locked in a tower. He has a chat open there, too, and he's sent pictures to some of the girls. I wonder how old they are, how old he thinks they are, or should be. Some of them have little $x$'s next to their names—they've blocked him, it says when I hover over their boxes—but there are others. I know there will always be others.

I throw up bile into the empty trash can at the side of his desk. Before, there was always a chance it was just my history, just his dad, just my imagination. But this is a pattern I know, one I've lived and seen over and over and never been able to stop in time.

I gag again over the trash can and think of Sebastian, this man I don't know, even though I know what he's done. Even though I knew, even when he young, that it might come to this.

I run away, still holding the trash can, and don't stop until I've locked my bedroom door behind me.

# 62

*Sam*

Thursday morning, I wait at my desk for Stubsen. His voice is deeper than usual as he delegates routes for the patrol guys. He's in charge while Baer's taking his two weeks in Florida, and these few minutes give me a chance to regroup each morning before he comes over.

"Hey Ellis," he says when he's finished with the others. "You want another coffee today?"

"Absolutely." I smile at him. This is like being undercover, I think, like something from one of his TV shows. Most of us are undercover, I guess, one way or another.

When he comes back with a coffee mug, his French vanilla energy powder already mixed in, I have my phone out by my keyboard. So he sees it light up and buzz against the wood at eight fifteen, when Lisa calls.

I apologize and roll my eyes, pointing to the caller ID. "It's Lisa," I tell him. "She's going through a bad breakup, and right before her birthday. I'd better get this."

I don't answer the phone until I'm out in the hallway and Stubsen's sliding off my desk.

"On time?" Lisa asks as soon as I pick up.

"Perfect," I tell her.

"Good. So they're good samples," she says. "I can run the mugs."

I catch my reflection in the glass, then look through it, at Stubsen loitering around the kitchen, waiting for me to come back.

"You gonna tell me whose they are?" Lisa asks.

I think about this. I really do.

"Is one of them Rolenfeld?"

"One of them," I admit, turning away from the window.

Lisa whistles. "Wow. Okay. So still on for tomorrow?"

"Definitely." Because these weekends away are important. "I'll be there by eight-thirty," I tell her. "But call if you get the results before then, okay?"

"Gotcha," she says.

# 63



I pretend to be asleep as Brent's getting ready to go into work Friday morning. I flip to my other side while he's in the shower and try to keep my breathing slow when I feel his breath on my cheek.

I finally sit up when I hear his truck pull away. It's louder now in the cold. The room's colder than usual, too, I think, but maybe this is just me, the newness of waking up these last couple mornings with someone in the bed next to me.

I remind myself we've done this before, even squeezed into extra long twin beds together during college visits and slept on so many sofas after late night movies over the years. Nothing else happened; he just followed me up here Wednesday night like this was normal. But now things are different. I can't wrap my head around how, around what exactly's changed between us. It feels almost like we're little again and playing house. But we're not little anymore, and this house is real.

I lie down for a while longer and watch the blue fade into the windows. There's a dusting of snow that came through the night, but it will melt soon.

I've been sleeping through the mornings this week, but today, I want to get out of the bed, to get out of the house. I remember I could use some groceries before Gleson's gets crowded over the weekend, so I throw on a pair of yoga pants and skip breakfast.

I pull my hair into a ponytail at the stoplight on Meridian that lasts too long for there not being any cars on the road and get to Gleson's a little before nine. Then I go for the usual things I can count and some syrup and mix for pancakes. Maybe I'll make them for Cody this weekend, since he's been doing so much cooking.

I'm almost to the checkout lane when I see Leah Schulz. I recognize her right away from all the Social pictures I shouldn't have scrolled through. And this is Paige, so I can't just walk by her. That's what I tell myself, anyway. But maybe it's all the pretending I've been doing lately that's catching up with me.

She turns when I call her name and doesn't move as I wheel my cart up to hers, the way you visit in these aisles. It seems like no one else is here yet, no beeping at the checkout counters or opening and closing of freezer doors. Behind us, there's just one employee milling around the produce department while he looks at his phone.

I don't know what to say to Leah at first, so I tell her I like her sweater.

She thanks me, but she's looking over my shoulder.

"Are you off work today?" I ask.

"I'm transferring," she says. Her eyes drop to a box of cereal in her cart. "I start next week."

"Why?" I don't remember this isn't any of my business until it's out of my mouth.

"Just another opportunity," she says to the cereal. "These internships are usually short-term."

"Sure," I say. "That's great." But that's not what I mean, either, that she should go, should get away from Brent. "Where?"

"Felden. The catalog place."

"Oh. They're great people, you know. The Leeson's are my neighbors."

She finally looks at me but doesn't say anything.

"So how was the concert?" I ask when we've been standing here for too long.

"Concert?" she says it like Kym Hartmann did, with the same little half-frown frown Kym's always had. Maybe Leah picked it up from her.

"In the city," I say. "I forget the band. It was a new one, wasn't it?"

"I don't know what you're talking about."

"A couple weeks ago. Saturday."

I think recognition's about to dawn on her face and she's going to smile. But her face doesn't change. "I'm sorry," she says.

"Sorry?" I'm not sure what she's sorry for. Does she know something about me and Brent and feel guilty about this? Of course that's probably it. Probably I should feel something about this, too.

"I don't know what you're talking about," she says.

"You didn't go to a concert with Brent? In Columbus?"

She takes a step back. "With Brent?" she asks.

"I didn't mean like as..." I don't know what I didn't mean. So we just stand here for a few seconds listening to footsteps in the next aisle.

"We're not friends," Leah offers after the footsteps have disappeared.

Not friends. *More*, I wonder? *Less*, it looks like now. "You're angry with him?" I ask, even though this isn't any of my business, either. And I don't know why it takes me so long to start apologizing.

I keep going until a woman's voice comes over the speakers calling someone to the bakery.


I can't stop thinking about Leah the rest of the day. It's a funny guessing game—either Brent or Leah lying, with no real reason for either of them to lie to me.

Maybe Leah's angry with him now, if he broke something off with her. Maybe there was more to break off than he let on. And I don't know Leah well enough to know what she's like when she's into someone, if she's competitive or clingy or one of those indifferent-acting women who actually aren't indifferent at all. I don't know anything about her at all, really. I don't even remember which community college Brent said she came from.

I should have asked more questions, should have paid more attention. I'm still thinking about it, wondering what I missed, when he texts me a little before five.

*Almost off*, he says. *On my way in a few.*

I don't have to think about this. *Don't*, I say, then, *I think I'm coming down with something.*

*What?*

It's the first time I've lied to him—really lied, not just left something out. *Maybe I got what your mom's had,* I say.

The dots flash for a second before they disappear.

It's not long afterwards that Cody texts.

*Brent staying again?* he asks.

*No,* I write. *Not tonight.* Maybe not again. Maybe this is over now, whatever it's been all these years or was turning into these last few days.

*Shoot,* Cody says. *I'm still in Dale. The supplier wasn't here, and I'm running late. I'll get back as fast as I can.*

*I'm okay,* I tell him, and think this is probably true.

Then he calls. I pick up right away.

"I'll leave right now," he says. "So maybe seven-thirty?"

"Sure. I'll set the alarm and turn on the lights. The other nights, nothing's happened before ten." I say it like this thing in my head is real and can only happen at certain times.

"Kay," he says. "See you then."

# 64

*Sebastian*

I put my phone in my pocket and think about how easy it is to hate her—to hate all the *hers*, really, for everything they do to us.

The parking lot's dark now, and I pace between the rows thinking about what I'm going to do.

I have a tack with me, one of those big, flat ones I've been saving for a while, holding onto in case I needed it someday. I shove it under the front tire of a white SUV, then get ready for Kara.

# 65



*Sam*


I've been on the road to Cincinnati for over an hour when my cell phone rings.

"You're on your way?" Lisa asks as soon as I pick up.

I tell her I left late but should still be there by eight-thirty.

"Okay," she says, but her voice isn't right. "I'm sorry. I think you won't like this. I got the tests back, and the DNA isn't a match."

"For which one? Stubsen or Rolenfeld?"

"Stubsen," she says, her voice distant. "I thought it might have been his. But it's not either of them."

It takes a breath for me to see it, for my stomach to drop and the highway between the two empty cornfields to blur in front of me.

Lisa's quiet as I pull over onto the rumble strip.

"You're sure?" I ask.

"Yeah. I'd say they have similar genetic backgrounds to the kit, but I bet you knew that already."

I set the phone down and put it on speaker. My fingers don't want to press the buttons, and there are a couple beeps as I accidentally hit some number keys.

"I'm sorry," I start.

"You have to get back there," she guesses. "You know who it is."

I put the car in gear again. There's a turnaround about a mile away.

"You know who it is," Lisa repeats.

"I do," I say, and gun it for the turnaround.

# 66

*Kara*

It's the feeling of being alone, or maybe just knowing it that gets me. That must be why I hear things—outside, first, rustling, probably a raccoon or a squirrel.

I go upstairs and turn on the TV. *Golden Girls* won't be on for a while, so I click over to the house channel, another renovation. It should distract me, I think, should keep my mind on houses instead of on these things I hear in my head and Leah and Brent and whatever we are now that's turned me into a liar, too.

I look at the nightstand clock. It's 7:15; Cody will be here soon, maybe even in time for the big reveal at the end of the show. It's just some new tile and landscaping and a couple commercials away.

I focus on the show, and when I hear the crickets—all at once, this time, and loud—I remind myself they're in my head. They have to be; the ground's frozen after last night's snow. But they just keep getting louder.

I turn off the TV when I can't stand it anymore, then open the door and flip on all the house lights I can reach like the light might make them quiet.

They don't stop. I run down the stairs. My breath catches at the bottom, when it's just my reflection in the mirror. I must have thought I'd see something behind me.

I cross the living room and hit the switch for the outside lights. The wind's blown a few leaves across the deck. That's something I can see, the leaves and the giant maple and the edge of the floodlight in the corner. And the sofa and the coffee table. That's five. I can feel my heartbeat, the blood rushing through my legs like I'm going to run—what *from* I don't know. I know I can't outrun this.

I can feel the tile under my feet when I get to the kitchen, the brush of my sleeves across my wrists, the vents blowing warm air over my ankles.

But all I hear are the crickets.

I sit down at the table and wait. I'm not sure what for. I breathe, hold my fingers like I used to, start tapping on pressure points and imagining this screaming in my head fading away.

It doesn't. Then the house goes dark.

# 67



*Sam*

I've just passed the county line when my phone rings again. I think it's going to be Lisa, at first, telling me she's made a mistake and the DNA's a match for Stubsen or Rolenfeld after all. I want her to have made a mistake, just this once. But it's Kara.

I hear the crickets as soon as I slide the toggle.

"Kara?

She's breathing hard, but it's the crickets that make my foot flatten on the accelerator two miles from the exit.

"Kara, I hear them. I hear the crickets," I tell her, trying to keep my voice steady. "Can you tell me where you are?"

There's a beat, a couple breaths. "Upstairs." Her voice is soft. "The bedroom."

"Does that door lock?"

She says something I can't make out.

"Kara, I'm calling this in. The police will be there as soon as they can."

The line's quiet.

"I'm going to be there soon, okay? I'm on my way. But first, I need you to lock the bedroom door."

"The doors," she says. "I locked..."

She cuts out for a second. I don't know what to say. I could tell her to stay calm, I guess. That's what people always say, like anyone's ever been calm because someone told them to be. But she shouldn't be calm. He has a key.

"The security system," she says. "The light's green. I set it. It was red. But then the power went out, the whole house, and..."

"That's okay," I tell her, because the security system doesn't matter, either. He has the code. "I want you to lock the bedroom door with you inside. Do you understand?"

"The door," she says. Her voice sounds like it's far away, like she's holding the phone away from her face.

"And do you have a chair? Or a desk or anything up there?" I should be able to remember. I should have paid more attention when I went up to get her phone.

"A chair," she says, her voice a little stronger this time. She's not panicking, I think, and I want to write this—*NOT PANICKING*—all over her fucking file.

"Okay," I say. "I want you to wedge it under the door handle to keep it from being pushed open."

There's a noise.

"Kara? I'm almost there."

The phone beeps. She's hung up.

# 68



*Kara*

I should be moving faster. It feels like my legs are too heavy, like I'm walking through something more than just air. I reach towards the wall in the darkness, the crickets still screaming in my head.

The stun gun hurts my hand. I'm squeezing it tight, like maybe it's going to do something. Like maybe this isn't just in my head.

I don't know why I'm not moving faster. I was walking normally, I think, when I went to get the stun gun from the nightstand.

My phone's on the floor now somewhere around the bed. It's gone dark, too, dead. There's just the green light on the far wall—the security system that's not set anymore, since the power went off. Everything around it's dark. I should be able to get to it, if I could move faster.

But it takes so long for me to cross the room and press the "arm" button, and then the system takes longer than the few seconds it should to light up. The beep's quiet when it does.

Nothing can compete with the crickets.

When I go for the chair, I'm finally moving faster. I can barely make out the floral pattern in the moonlight, and I stub my toes into the sides as I scoot it along the carpet. I'm closing the door when it runs into something.

A thing, I think. Not a person. Just a shadow slinking through the darkness.

But it grabs me, and then we're on the floor, rolling.

I won't win. I can tell right away, with my legs kicking and my throat trying to scream and not being able to. It pins me down.

When I get an arm loose, I squeeze the stun gun. The red light's between me and it, and I press the button.

There's crackling, a jolt of blue sparks.

*Push the slider. Press "stun." Hold for no more than three seconds.*

But I don't think about the three seconds until the sparks have run out. By then, neither of us are moving.

# 69

Cody's making good time. He's almost to the town line when he sees a white SUV across the road. It's pulled off sideways with its headlights shining into the cornfield.

He pulls over, like you do in places like Paige, and flips on his hazards. He doesn't have to look to cross the street; this is a long stretch of back road that's always quiet at night.

He walks into the glow of the headlights. A woman's kneeling in the grass and trying to push a lift behind the driver's side tire. She sits up when she sees him, looks around like she might go somewhere.

Cody stays several paces away. "It's Leah, isn't it?" he asks. "You work with Kym Hartmann and Brent Thomas?"

She doesn't move, doesn't say anything right away.

"I'm Cody Muller. Looks like you've got a flat?"

"Yeah." Her shoulders drop then, and she looks behind her, down the road. "I don't know what happened. The wheel just jerked."

"That can happen," Cody tells her. He steps to the side of the headlights where he can see, but he doesn't get any closer.

She starts to say something about the lift. Her face is red from the cold, and she's shaking a little.

"You know," he says, "I've been wantin' to time myself at that. Haven't had a flat in a while. Why don't I do it? You could wait in the car."

Leah starts to protest, but it's not long before she climbs into the driver's seat, shivering. Then Cody closes the door behind her, kneels down, and gets to work.

# 70

*Kara*

I'm lying on the floor, my hand in something wet. I don't know what it is or how long it's been there.

There's a light. Someone says my name.

It's under me, the thing I think isn't even a person. But when the light shines down on it, I can see its soft middle, its eyes open, those warm brown orbs like a cocker spaniel.

There's a siren now, but the crickets have all stopped.

# 71


*Sam*


She's sitting over him, the stun gun still in her hand. Her other hand's shaking his shoulder like he might wake up.

I think of what the others will see when they get up here, what I'll have to put in the report. His ski mask must have gotten pushed up in the struggle. There's vomit running off this side of his chest and into the carpet.

"Kara," I say again.

She hasn't noticed me yet. She didn't react to the sirens, either. I think she won't for a while.

She's talking, but not to me. She doesn't know why he won't say anything, why he isn't moving. His eyes are still open, but he's paralyzed from the stun gun.

I look at the door, at the flashing red and blue lights along the living room wall, then back at Kara. We don't have much time. Stubsen and one of the other guys pulled in right behind me. They were ready to break down the door, but he'd left it open.

I sent them to her bedroom, the one where Cody's been staying, so I'd be up here first. It won't take them another minute to climb the stairs.

"Kara," I say. "I just want to take something from your hand. Is that okay?"

She doesn't move. She's still looking at him, still talking to him.

I squat down and set the flashlight to the side, then reach for her hand. "Kara, I'm just going to get this out of the way, okay? I'm not going to hurt you."

She doesn't move as I pry the little block from her fingers, and then I step back and keep talking to her. If she's lucky, she won't remember any of this.

I manage to push the stun gun under the armchair in the middle of the room just as Stubsen's coming through the door. I straighten and stop him as he lunges forward.

"An ambulance," I say, pushing at his chest.

Stubsen looks at me. His mouth's open like he's never seen something like this before. Maybe he hasn't ever seen something like this this before.

"Two," he says. "Two ambulances."

"One," I say, because I know what hospitals are like when you're coming out of shock.

Stubsen's eyes are wild, darting around. "Is there blood? There's..."

"A heart attack," I tell him. "It was a heart attack."

"She's not hurt? Kara, are you..." He shuts up when I shove him back.

"It's shock." The threat's passed now, at least. She just needs the time to see it, to process everything. She'll probably be lying there in the vomit for a while. She won't see me or anyone else until she's ready.

He reaches for her again. "Kara..."

I step in front of him, moving him back. "She's not hurt," I say. "I'll take her to the hospital if she needs it. Just get him out of here. That's priority one. Do you understand?"

Stubsen finally steps out into the hallway to call an ambulance. I can hear one of the deputies downstairs yelling over the beeping as he presses buttons on the house alarm and tries to talk to the dispatcher at the security company.

I look at Brent. He must have set the system behind him so he'd know if Kara tried to run.

Cody gets here just before the ambulance does. He comes bounding up the steps, and I don't do anything to stop him when he gets to us.

I fish the stun gun out from under the armchair and hand it to him when Stubsen's on the other side of the door directing the EMT's this way.

Cody takes it without saying anything, then steps back into the shadows by the bed.

This will all look better when they get the lights on, I tell Kara. I'm not sure whether she hears me. When the EMT's come in, I have to pry her off Brent. I pull from behind her, being careful not to pin her arms, and she falls back into me.

They ask me questions as they put him on the board, about his pulse and his breathing, and I make it sound like I've checked these things. They're getting a pulse, at least. He's alive.

And I think, as I'm watching them turn the gurney through the doorway and Kara's gone slack and quiet against me, that I could have done it. One more shock probably would have been enough, and then all of this would have been over.

# 72



Friday night bleeds into Saturday afternoon. It's quiet at Kara's with just us here and a deputy dropping by every now and then. There's not much news.

I don't know how the time goes for Kara. She's still living it, I think, will stay stuck in these memories for as long as she stays in this house. So I won't blame her for taking off soon. At the beginning, they're always a little like stunned birds who have just run into a window. It takes a while to come back to themselves, but they all get away as soon as they can.

Cody got the power back on quickly. It was just a flipped breaker—easy to do, if you knew the house as well as Brent did—and I've fielded a few calls this morning about the sound machine that was found on the North side of the house. It was hooked up to some speakers he put under her bedroom. You can see the road from that clump of trees, so Brent must have always been able to see when Cody or I were coming and turned it off in time.

I should have assumed the sound machine. I should have

known who Sebastian was, too, as soon as I saw the Disney movies in the media cabinet that night we brought Kara home from the gala. It's almost too cute of an alias—the patient friend, the lobster he thought should have been Ariel's prince, instead.

I glance back at Kara as I talk to one of the deputies at the door. She's sitting at the kitchen island having more coffee. This is what she's done all night, like if she just drinks enough coffee, everything else will go back to normal, too.

"So the hospital says he's conscious now," Ron tells me, shifting on his feet and trying to see inside. It was easy for me to take charge when it happened. Just seeing Kara and Brent lying on the carpet was enough to shake Stubsen.

I thank Ron and tell him he can go.

"You want me to go see him, or..."

"We don't need a statement," I say. "Not yet."

Ron doesn't move. "You don't want me to go get..."

"No," I say, harder this time, because we have everything we need for now from Kara. Her statement didn't even take long once she understood what had happened.

She stayed calm, working through the times she thought she was imagining things—when she'd heard crickets or there was a light she didn't remember turning on or a drink she didn't remember taking or a lotion she didn't remember setting out. That was Brent's game, making her feel so crazy she'd think she could only have him and so unsafe when he wasn't here that she'd beg him to stay.

The head of cardiology at the hospital says he's going to make it. He'll be there few more days for observation. So I'll wait until Monday to go, saying I'm just letting him recover. I want him to sweat.

He had a heart attack, but there wasn't a good reason for it, Dr. Kemper said when I talked to him around four this morning. Except there was a pretty good reason, in Brent's case, those burn marks on his chest suggest. But those pictures will go straight into my desk first thing on Monday. They don't need to be in the writeup Baer will get when he gets back. They don't have anything to do with what really happened.

Cody stayed through the early hours of this morning and has been in and out all day. He's picked up food from what must be every place in town by now, just bringing it by and leaving it out on the island like Kara might see something she likes and eat it without thinking. She did, for a while, nibbled on some sliders from Hubbuch's while she was staring out the windows, so I guess he was right.

A little while later, she starts moving around more. She has questions, but not as many of them as I thought she would. I try to answer them as objectively as I can. There's conflicting advice on how to handle this, on how much information someone can deal with when they're coming out of a traumatic experience. I think it's best to know the truth upfront, so that's what I give her.

Cody's back in the driveway when she decides she's ready to go. So he packs her truck with coolers full of all the foods he's picked up, and I get some of her things from the upstairs bedroom while she's circling around the living area.

There's still vomit on the carpet up here, and the room looks wrong with sun streaming in through the curtains. I bring down some clothes and a few things she had in that bathroom.

Then we let her go.

She's surprised, I think, that we don't try to argue with her, to give her some reason to stay. But these aren't the kinds of memories that will wash away with the spring rains and the layers of leaves that mold down into the woods and the blizzards that blanket the place in peace. Sometimes, I know, it's better to leave a place behind.

*     *

Sunday morning, Cody and I are back at The Strawberry at our usual time, ordering my eggs and his bacon and sunny sides and hashbrowns like Friday night never happened. Though I'm getting more interested glances from the waitresses than hostile ones today. The place is busier than usual, too, between the church seatings. It's been a big weekend for Paige; people have a lot to talk about.

Cody managed to snag a booth in the far corner by the kitchens. It's separated from the others by a hallway, so it at least feels more private.

"You've heard from Kara again?" he asks once our waitress— Madison Fuhs again, UL, dance team—is a safe distance away. "She's okay?"

I spread some extra grape jam on my toast and wonder if I need to start watching my sugar here. "She is," I say. "She wanted me to thank you for the food." When I talked to her this morning, she told me he packed Stan's truck so full of takeout that she had to throw out everything she'd left in her fridge back home to make room.

"You'll keep her updated?" Cody's still tense. He blames himself for not getting back to the house in time. He thinks he should have been there as soon as it was even starting to get dark, before the power was turned off, and then he would have gotten to Brent first. There was only so much I could say to convince him the time of day wasn't the important variable. It's always the rapist.

"She doesn't want to know about Brent," I tell him. And I think she chose that right. You can obsess about these things, can stay in the loop on every little detail, but it doesn't always help. *Let the monster die*, as my old commander used to say. Though I haven't known anyone who could actually do that, at least not until their monster was caught or dead.

"You can keep her updated on the house," I tell Cody, "once she's settled in a little."

"I wasn't sure if I should call or..."

I watch as he scrapes the butter knife across his toast. I've watched him for a while with Kara, how slowly he moves around her and how he's always known not to invade her space.

"It's okay," I tell him. "She's a lot better. Considering the time, I mean."

"Yeah?" He looks up. "You know what's supposed to happen now? You've seen it before?"

"We've all seen it before."

He shakes his head. "I don't mean him breaking in and cutting the power. I mean the rape, and then him..." He doesn't know how to finish this. But Cody's always been able to say the word 'rape,' has always been able to call it what it is. Maybe this is a sign, a way to tell his type from the ones you have to watch out for.

I set down my toast and try to explain how this works, the statistics, the one in three women and all the rape kits that never even get run—Kara Peterson's will be an exception, properly this time—and all the other things we don't talk about. It's happened to me, to lots of people he knows. But Kara will be better back in Columbus. This was her closure; her monster has a name now. And this monster, I'll get.

Cody's face is as tight as the rest of him when I finish, and he sits there for a while before he responds, long enough for me to get in a couple bites of toast.

"Brent'll go to jail, though," he says, finally.

"We don't even have him on breaking and entering. He had a key, and he knew the alarm code. But the sound machine's enough to get a warrant for his DNA to run against the rape kit."

"And then? When they prosecute..."

"*If* they prosecute," I correct, "it probably still won't be jail time." You can get pretty good at estimating these sentences by race and years that have passed, community size and reputation. Brent will have a bunch of character witnesses and plausible drunkenness and his age on his side for the rape. That's if it goes to court. It probably won't. And then he'd say Friday night was a sex game, I bet, or a joke. That's what they usually say.

"That's bullshit." Cody's stopped even pretending he's going to eat his toast.

I nod. I take a sip of my tea, lukewarm like usual here.

"What about Rolenfeld? I heard Ron say he's untouchable, but..."

There's no good *but* here. I try to swallow this feeling that always comes with the cases you can't see an end to. Dalton will always be out there. Even when he slips up the next time—and there are always next times for people like Dalton—nothing will stick to him. This was about power, about knowing exactly how much he could get away with, and he called it right.

"I think Ron's right about that," I say.

"You don't think with Brent sayin' in court, about him..." Cody wants to say *holding her down*, but he can't. His knuckles are white against the table, braced on either side of him.

I shake my head. "Dalton could give him whatever he wants. We could offer Brent a plea deal to implicate him, but they're the only witnesses, and Brent knows he'd probably get off with some light community service, if anything, if it even went to trial."

"But you know what he was gonna do when he got to her," Cody says. "You know..."

"He was wearing a ski mask, but he didn't break in."

Cody opens his mouth, but I interrupt him.

"And we don't know. Not really." And a rape Friday night wouldn't be any more likely to be prosecuted than the one ten years ago was.

"He could have killed her."

"You think so?" I ask. *I* think so, of course but it seems like most people don't, until it happens. No one ever sees these things coming, and then they don't say "mental illness" or "incel" or whatever. They say it must have been about passion, that these are crimes of passion. They're always wrong. These are always crimes of control.

"If he could do all that. A fucking sound machine. If he was fucking with her like that, then you know..." Cody's voice trails off. It's gone cold, a Cody I don't recognize, like the 'fucking.' But this rage is different than Brent's. It's a subtle difference, I think, one it really takes a situation like this one to see.

"I agree with you," I say. But that's how it always is. It's a pretty subtle difference, too, between hate and what some people say is love.

# 73


*Kara*


I thought nights would be different now. I don't know what I was expecting would get me when I walked into my apartment yesterday, but nothing did. I took a Benadryl and slept straight through the morning. Tonight, I don't even think I need the Benadryl. But maybe I'm wrong; maybe these things can come back.

I think it would be different if I'd stayed in Paige, tried to sleep in that bedroom where I laid in Brent's vomit and watched his eyes stuck open, staring at me. I don't feel anything when I remember it yet, but that can happen, they say. You go numb to it for a while, until it comes back—slowly, hopefully, and not all at once like the crickets that went from nothing to screaming. But that was just a sound machine.

Cody told me he'd handle everything with the house to get it on the market. Maybe I can come back when it's winter to sign the papers, he said, if it goes quickly, so at least there won't be any real crickets outside.

I microwave one of the enchiladas from Pedro's that he packed for me and bring it over to the sofa. This is where I sat with Brent just after we got the note and made plans to come home. His note. I should have known, but that's what Sam said would happen, too, that everyone thinks they should have known things they couldn't have. She told me *she* should have seen it, though; the handwriting looked a lot like mine, and there were only so many people who would have been able to imitate me.

I sit and eat. Through these walls, I can hear a laugh every now and then from my neighbors with the seven year old, and tonight, I catch a whiff of spicy curry from the family on the other side. It never gets to be too much, being packed in like this, and I wonder if I'm a herd animal now, if I feel safer with others around me and only these thin walls between us. The lights illuminate the lawn all the way to the highway. It's never dark here.

I get out my laptop, but there's nothing to do, no work for most of the rest of the year. I start to turn on the TV, then put down the remote.

I open the laptop and look at my calendar, but the weeks ahead of me are all blank.

# 74



*Sam*

I'm surprised when Stubsen beats me to the station Monday morning.

"Turner okayed it," he says as soon as the door swings shut behind me. "The judge. We can get DNA from Brent and send it and the kit to get tested, but the kit's not where it's supposed to be, and..."

"I already sent it."

Stubsen opens his mouth and just looks at me for a second. "You sent it?"

"To Cincinnati," I tell him. "To my friend there, Lisa. I picked it up Saturday night so she could run it as soon as we got approval. She'll be faster than Columbus. Cheaper, too."

Stubsen doesn't move. I walk around him.

"Oh," he says. "Good. That's...good. Thank you."

I look around at the rest of the guys, all quiet today and heading straight out instead of socializing in the kitchen. It smells like coffee like always, but Stubsen isn't holding any as he follows me to my desk. He must have already had his. Though his usual mug's still missing. I should probably feel bad about this, but I'll get it back tomorrow, maybe shove it to the back of the sugar cabinet and find it again. He'll never know it left.

"So what I need to do is get a sample," he says. He looks at his usual corner of my desk but doesn't sit down. "A DNA sample from Brent."

I focus on some papers in my bin, new ones from the hospital that Ron must have brought by yesterday. "You think you can do that?" I ask. I think for a second after that I might apologize, tell him it's been a long weekend. But I don't.

Stubsen just stands there. I set the papers down.

"I'll go with you to the hospital," I say.

"I know I screwed this up," he says. "It's just..."

He stops when I look at him—*really* look at him, not like I'm trying to catch a rapist or a murderer anymore, but like there are other things that can be almost as wrong with a man.

"You were right about her. Kara," he says. "I guess I missed the mark on this one."

He meets my eyes, and after a second, I nod.

"So I'll go with you," I repeat, "to the hospital."

"Thank you," he says, and then he goes away.

A little after ten, I'm waiting under all the bright fluorescent lights in the hallway of the Rolenfeld extension as Stubsen collects a saliva sample from Brent Thomas. Bev's not in today, and the other nurses are all tiptoeing along the pale blue terrazzo and peeking around corners to this little alcove when they pass by.

Stubsen won't be long. He had the warrant ready to go well before we left the station. It's like he's a different person today. He had questions on the ride over about the case, too, about the things he missed at the beginning and shouldn't have.

When he comes back out to the hallway, he looks like he's seen a ghost, and I tell him to go downstairs without me. I want just a few minutes alone with Brent. With any luck, a few minutes are all I'll need.

Stubsen starts to protest, saying he'll stay, but I convince him to go to the front desk to collect some medical records, instead. We don't really need a physical copy, but this will keep him busy for a while.

"I'll get a ride back with Cody, actually," I tell him. "I'm off now, and he was planning to meet me here."

"Oh," Stubsen says, then, "of course."

"I have my cell if you need me. And I'll be in tomorrow to finish the report."

He nods and stands there for a second before he goes.

I wait until he's down the hallway and around the corner before I walk into Brent's room.

"I guess your mom's not coming into work this week," I say as I close the door behind me, to lead with something that might get him.

Brent's face doesn't change. Probably I should have expected this, though; his mom's a woman, too, likely the same as any other to him.

My stomach sinks as I hold his eyes. He looks calm, like he's been all the other times I've seen him—running up to Kara outside the gala, covering her in blankets, getting her water from the kitchen sink. But there's a little smile that creeps in at the corners of his mouth now. People like Brent and Dalton can't stop this smile when they think they're getting away with something.

I look around the room and try to seem disinterested, but my hands are sweating, and I can feel my pulse in my fingertips. So I count things I can see, like Kara told me she does—the oak tree outside the window that's lost almost all its leaves. The navy blanket laid out over the foot of the bed. The little TV in the corner, on mute on some daytime talk show. The red chair pushed up against the wall. It hasn't been pulled out; no one's been to visit him. The IV in his left arm, probably just fluids at this point. The supervising nurse said he should be released tomorrow. We'll hold him, of course, and process him, but I'm sure he'll be bailed within the hour, and who knows how long it will be then before there's any talk of a prosecution.

"The doctors don't know how it happened," he says, when I don't expect him to say anything. "The heart attack."

I pull the curtain around, blocking the view from the door, and sit down. "You'd be surprised how easily hearts can break," I tell him. "A little caffeine. A little excitement. You don't even need a medical history."

Brent doesn't respond. I fold my hands in my lap to keep from touching the pocket with the microphone in it.

"I guess Dalton hasn't been to visit you," I say. "You haven't had any visitors at all, have you? Doesn't bode great for the trial."

His face doesn't move. It's like he was meant to be stunned, to be immobilized the way he was Friday night. One more shock, I keep thinking. It would have been enough. I don't know why I didn't do it.

"Though that won't matter, I guess, with your DNA," I say. "Kara Peterson's rape kit's finally being processed."

He leans forward. "You really think so?" His voice is steady. "You really think with Rolenfeld's name in the capitol..."

"Oh, it didn't go to Columbus. I sent it to my friend in Cincinnati. She's faster."

Brent's lip twitches, barely.

"But I don't want you to worry about Kara while your heart's in delicate shape. She's fine. She won't have to come back for the trial or anything."

"There isn't gonna be a trial."

My smile comes easy this time. This is it, almost where I want him. "Maybe not," I say. "I wondered if you'd let it get that far."

When I look at him now, he looks like someone else. Who we should have seen him for all along, obviously. Who *I* should have seen him for, at least.

He's about to say something about how he won't kill himself, how he'll take his chances with the system, and I know I have to stop him before he can hear himself make these promises.

"But I guess she'll probably be coming back some anyway," I say, "for Cody." My voice isn't as strong this time, and I worry Brent sees through me. This was Cody's idea. He thought it might redirect some of the anger away from Kara, making Brent go after him, instead.

Brent shifts. The bed creaks. "No," he says.

"No?"

His face is totally unrecognizable. I've seen this before, though. It's why you can't always identify someone afterwards when they're in a lineup. They look so different when they're like this.

"Bullshit." Spit flies out of his mouth. "He's with you."

This one throws me. *Me and Cody?* I laugh, a little, for real.

Then I pull Brent's phone out of my pocket, the clone he made of Kara's that's still getting all her text messages. Even the extra ones I had her send Cody this morning. The malware for Brent's program must have been why her battery kept dying; Ron said it takes a lot of energy to send a signal to the clone all the time.

"I guess I could show you," I say.

He makes a grab for it, rolls to his side and into the rail of the bed, but I'm faster. The tape from his IV pulls off his elbow.

"You can't use that as evidence," he says. "I know you can't."

"I can," I tell him, holding it up. "We had a warrant for it this morning. It was with your hospital things. In your pocket. Do you want to see her texts with Cody? He was there right away, you know, after. Do you want to know what they..."

And that's it, is enough, just like Cody thought it would be. They say it's a blind rage, when someone like Brent shows you who they really are. They don't know what they're saying. It's not always admissible in a trial, but at least I understand, at the end of it, about Kara and about how he much he thinks he deserved her, about how she should have been his. Even about Stan. Stan, who he didn't have anything against. Killing him was just what he had to do to get Kara to come home. Just a little caffeine. Not difficult to get or anything. Nothing he regretted.

Of course the nurses all hear him, all of Bev's colleagues. When I pull back the curtain, two of them are there, wide-eyed, one of them holding a syringe.

I reach into my pocket to make sure the recording's still going. The green light's blinking, and I can't help my own smile as I walk out of the room, my heart pounding faster than I bet Brent's ever got Friday night.


Cody's waiting for me in the lobby, sitting in one of the big leather chairs and holding the local paper. He's not even pretending to read it. He stands as soon as he sees me and dumps it on the coffee table.

"He said it," I tell him.

"And Stan?"

I nod. "So that might be enough to hold him on once he's discharged." Because murder beats rape. Most everything does.

"Might?" I don't turn to look at his face, but Cody's voice is clipped, hard.

"It's a private recording," I say, "enough for a judge to hold him on for a bit, but it probably wouldn't be admissible in a trial."

Cody doesn't say anything as we walk out into the wind, but his arms are stiff at his sides. The skies are overcast, like they'll stay for the next several months, and some leaves blow up into my ankles as we pass the big sycamore in the circle.

"It worked, your idea," I tell him. "You were right about him being jealous. We might get lucky."

"You think he'll kill himself?"

"Maybe."

Cody doesn't say anything until we're across the parking lot. "So that's it?" he asks then. "That's all we can do?"

"That's it," I say, and climb up into his truck.

*     *

I have Bev bring in Brent's computer Tuesday morning to see what we might get from it, but he's dead before it even makes it to the judge.

# 75

Bev

One month later

The townhouse I'm renting looks out over Lake Eerie, the yard a grassy hill that drops off into sand and waves and driftwood. I've decided I like the sound of the water behind me. The noise sends me to sleep most nights and stays with me on my morning walks.

The women's clinic's just down the street, and I volunteer for every open shift. I thought it was just to take my mind off things at the beginning, that I was running away, but it feels right now. *I feel right here.*

I don't hide my scar anymore. These scars are something a lot of us have in common, and I think it helps the patients see me as someone like them, someone who can help.

The other nurses only know that my son died and that I'm a widow who's new to the area. They like to ask me how I'm holding up. Maybe one day I'll tell them why they shouldn't feel sorry for me, why this isn't grief I'm going through. All I felt when Sam Ellis came to the house to tell me my son had killed himself was relief.

I still feel a pang when I think of Kara, and some nights I sit up wondering how I could possibly tell her everything. I've written a few letters I haven't sent. I just don't know where to start.

I knew what this looked like in my husband. I should have been able to catch it before Brent got too old. He wasn't quite thirteen when Branden died, and I used to tell myself, cooped up next door with Deb when the kids were at school, that it wasn't genetic. But I always wondered if he saw what really happened, what we told him afterwards was just an accident, and his father got into him then like a virus.

They said he asked to see me when he was in the hospital. I didn't go, and then he killed himself the same way he killed Stan, the same way I killed his father. So he must have known that much, at least. The caffeine pills were Deb's idea, and she maintained until the day she died that it was her best one. Stan had just been elected sheriff that year, so no one looked into Branden's death.

The sun's coming up now, and there's colder air blowing off the lake as I cross 33rd and weave through the parking lot of the donut place on the corner of King. I don't look over my shoulder anymore.

I worried at first that my demons would follow me here, but it's like they died as soon as I wasn't Branden's wife or Brent's mom anymore. Now, I'm someone else altogether, free of both of them.

# 76


*Kara*



*Three months later*


I'm struck by how normal The Strawberry looks at noon on a Saturday. I don't know why I thought it would be different.

Cody watches me from across the table as I eat my pancakes. Maybe I shouldn't have ordered them; I haven't had pancakes for a while, and they should remind me of Brent more than anything, but they don't. I guess it's that The Strawberry's taste different enough than the ones Brent and I used to make with our blueberries and chocolate chips.

Across the table, Sam asks me about my work—our busy season, with taxes—and Columbus and everything else that isn't Paige, like I might realize I'm here all of a sudden and then revert back to how I was the last time she saw me. But I feel fine in this booth, like I used to.

It's probably because I haven't gone back to the house. That's what my therapist thought was important, not going in until I felt ready, like Brent's ghost might tackle me again as soon as I walk through the front door. I'm not sure if she's right or not, but I didn't want to test it. So Cody met me at Becky Lange's office as soon as I drove in. The buyers are new to Paige, a young couple from up near Cleveland who are setting up a chiropractor's office behind the K-mart.

"You look really good. Like you're doing well," Sam tells me when she runs out of subjects she's sure are safe to talk about. Things are still settling here in Paige, and no one really knows what's off limits when it comes to Brent and everything that happened.

I tell her I *am* doing well and mean this.

"I bet the Lewis couple's happy to move in," she says. "They've been at the extended stay for forever."

"They seemed great," I say. I almost wish I were here to get to know them. Paige is changing, slowly, getting younger. "They said they knew the clinic where Bev's volunteering. They're from a town over."

Sam glances at the table behind us, where the hostess is seating a family with a couple kids. "So you've talked to her?" she asks.

I nod. I wasn't sure how getting in touch with Bev would go. I'd been thinking about it for a couple months when I just picked up the phone last week and called her out of the blue. It turns out she left a few days after I did and hasn't been back, either. She had to get out of the house, she told me. Maybe that's a thing with houses after something like this happens. Maybe the trauma sticks to them, coats all the pipes and blooms behind the drywall like mold.

Sam had already told me how Brent killed himself. It was caffeine pills, but they couldn't prove how he'd gotten ahold of them. It was right after they took him from the hospital—Dalton had just been to visit—as they were starting to process him at the station. The caffeine caused another heart attack, and the hospital couldn't save him that time. So I wasn't really surprised when Sam showed me my dad's autopsy report with the caffeine, and maybe I wasn't that surprised, either, when Bev told me about her husband. I should have known her accident when we were little wasn't an accident, that her scars were deeper than I saw. She told me about how my mom helped her, too, how it was Mom who got that first set of caffeine pills.

"Her plants are doin' good," Cody says when none of us have said anything for a while. He took them in for her, Bev told me, when she left.

"You know we saged them," Sam adds. She laughs, then, and I do, too, because I can imagine Cody following her around his place with a big sage smudge. That's something I read about in the blogs, how some people chase away bad energy with sage and fire and positive intentions like you don't actually have to kill it first. Or let it kill itself.

We're talking about Bev's ivy I remember hiding my broccoli in as a little kid when Parker and Becky Lange stop by our booth.

Becky presses my hand and says she's been praying for me, and Parker pats at my shoulder in a public display of support. It's easy to support me now, of course, that Brent's killed himself and Dalton's dumped Parker and is with whoever he's with now in

Washington.

I say the things I've memorized about how well and how normal I am, the same things I've said to everyone else who's stopped by this table and pretended we've been friends through everything that's happened and that this is what I'm here for, their support.

When they go, Cody assures me Dalton's not due back from Washington for a while and that Robert and Maureen are in the Caymans. But Dalton's been gone for me since Brent's death. I don't see his face anymore in my dreams. I know he planned it, or at least that he played a big role, but it was never really about him.

We make small talk with a few more people who stop by— with sympathy, or something like it—as I finish the rest of my pancakes.

"You'll come back?" Mrs. Merkel asks as she bends to give me a hug. "You're not gonna stay away forever now, are you?"

"I'm sure I'll come back," I tell her, and I wonder if this is true.

The sun's starting to break through the clouds by the time Cody walks me to my car. We pass over a grassy patch that separates The Strawberry's parking lot from the K-Mart. It's starting to get green already, even as I pull my coat tighter around me, ready for the first shoots of spring to push up through the bald patches of mud.

I thank Cody again. I don't know what else to say, and he's done so much. For the house and for me. He waves me off like usual and asks about the construction on 77 on my way back to the city. There's always construction on 77.

He waits while I climb into my car. "Can we keep in touch?" he asks.

I agree before he shuts the door and I drive away.

# 77

*Four years later*

Kara Peterson's driving down Meridian again, through the usual traffic at the end of the day with the factory letting out. A string of taillights is backed up all the way out to the junction.

She has a new SUV now, and Paige doesn't look the same to her from this seat. She traded in her car when she passed the Ohio bar, and it was just a couple months afterwards that her name was etched on the window of one of the old offices on the square. She knew right away she wanted it, the place on the corner that used to be an antique store owned by a childhood friend of her mom's. It's just a quick walk from there to The Strawberry and the old Victorian Sam's just finished renovating on Main.

Kara doesn't look at the Rolenfeld's land when she passes by. She keeps on going past the driveway to her old place before turning into the next one.

When she gets home, Cody's standing over the stove making tacos. He does this every Tuesday now.

She dumps her purse in the mud room and joins him in the kitchen. She thought it was weird, at first, that they'd end up in the

Leeson's old house, just a stone's throw from her dad's. But these are still her woods, quiet and carpeted in leaves now, just waiting on the next snow.

Martha had only lived there a couple years after the renovations when she decided she wanted to be closer to her grandson in Akron. She still visits every now and then, though, and couldn't be happier to see Cody and Kara in the house. Her conservatory's filled with a jungle of Bev's houseplants, all gone wild now, and Kara keeps up her roses in the garden. They'll provide the flowers for the wedding in a few months, big white and yellow ones from some of Martha's favorite bushes.

As Cody finishes making their plates, Kara steps out on the new deck. She likes to do this before dinner, even when it's cool. They have plans to get some outdoor chaises by summertime and a hammock, but tonight she just stands at the railing and looks out through the woods.

Cody's planted a few evergreens several yards back, at the border with the Rolenfeld's, so she can barely see the lake anymore. In a few years, the branches will block it out altogether.

www.ingramcontent.com/pod-product-compliance
Lightning Source LLC
Chambersburg PA
CBHW051214190726
48288CB00006B/1952